TEXAS COWBOY K9 PATROL

BARB HAN

Editing: Ali Williams

Cover Design: Jacob's Cover Designs

CHAPTER ONE

Rain came down in sheets, battering the half-built wooden deck on Lawson Quinn's townhouse. According to the forecast, the cold would come next. The early December heat wave was playing havoc with the weather as tornado alarms pierced through the boom of thunderclaps and the sound of the driving rain. As an officer who drove around in a vehicle for most of his shift, Lawson was used to Mother Nature's temper tantrums. For his K-9 partner, they'd taken some getting used to. In fact, Kodo had darn near been kicked out of the training program in San Antonio due to his fear of thunderstorms. That was not a desirable trait in a canine officer, nor was it realistic for the job. Based on Kodo's calm demeanor now, Lawson would never have guessed storms had ever been an issue for the Belgian Malinois.

Lawson parked his service vehicle and grabbed his bag from Velvet Taco before commanding Kodo to exit the sport utility. Tornadoes used to be confined to springtime. However, in recent years, they'd become more common leading up to and around Christmas.

Tucking his chin to his chest, he then bolted around his service vehicle to the side door of his townhouse. He splashed his way through puddles of water covering most of the stamped concrete walkway. He managed to get the key in, as needles of rain pounded the skin on his face. He unlocked the wood and glass door as a wind gust whooshed, practically snapping the handle out of his grasp. Kodo, at his side, was barely fazed by the bolt of lightning and almost immediate crack of thunder that signaled the storm was practically right on top of them. Lawson, on the other hand, was soaked and cranky.

Food and dry clothing might help. But first, he needed to take care of a few loose items on his patio before the wind got there first.

After setting the now-soggy bag on the countertop, Lawson immediately moved over to the sliding glass doors. He opened them just enough to slip out so he could secure the two-by-four wooden boards before they went flying through the air and ended up taking out a window. He'd known the rain was coming based on the rolling gray clouds from earlier, but the storm had picked up intensity while he was at the end of his shift and surprised him in how quickly it had turned ugly. Not only could he experience four seasons in a day this time of year, but the weather was as predictable as a squirrel darting across the street in midday traffic.

Kodo sat obediently at the door. Ears at attention, there were times when Lawson would swear that dog had human emotions on his face. Right now, he would bank on concern. Lawson gathered the two-by-fours that had been stacked on the ground and against the wall last weekend, when the weather was calm and it was predicted to stay that way. He rounded up the wood planks and then moved them inside the shed on his patio.

Once everything was secured, Lawson slipped back inside the townhouse and to a waiting Kodo. His canine buddy's tail immediately wagged as his snout popped up.

Despite knowing all the rules about eating first to remind Kodo who was dominant in the household, it didn't stop him from fixing Kodo's food bowl and then setting it down on the floor next to the table.

They were partners. They ate together. Period.

In this case, Kodo went first because Lawson needed to get out of his wet clothes. Changing into something dry and throwing his work clothes in the basket on top of the dryer took all of two minutes. Jeans and a t-shirt were more comfortable anyway.

Lawson polished off his pair of Korean BBQ tacos along with the chicken and waffle one. The plastic container had kept all three of them from becoming soaked along with the bag. He pulled a beer from the fridge, thinking about how much he was going to enjoy the next couple of hours as long as the weather didn't knock out power. He scratched Kodo behind the ears before reclaiming his seat at the table. Storms like these were mesmerizing. The wind howled. The rain pelted. And Mother Nature showed what she was capable of, reminding him and everyone else in her path that she was the one in charge, no matter how much anyone else believed otherwise. The minute she decided to flex, there was no question who was boss.

Thankfully, Kodo had already taken care of business after they left the station and before the deluge. That saved Lawson from having to take Kodo outside right now. Hopefully, this storm would blow over as fast as it came. The sudden, intense ones usually had a habit of doing just that and didn't cause too much harm. It was the big ones that stuck around, hovered, gained in intensity but didn't keep moving...those were trouble.

He checked the weather app on his cell phone. Uh-oh. The strength of the storm looked like it was about to double down. Much to his surprise, this one had just gained speed and morphed into the kind that would sit on top of them for a good number of hours yet.

Either way, Lawson was inside and hunkered down for a quiet evening after a busy shift.

"Good job today, Kodo," Lawson said, still thinking about the phone call from his brother Griff asking him to come home. Their father had a health issue that was serious enough for Lawson's older brother to believe they should all meet up to discuss the situation. Lawson wasn't close with his father, but he would make the trip home in the morning; not exactly the day off he had planned, but the situation at Quinnland seemed serious enough to warrant the trip.

The thought of Lawson's father being seriously ill wasn't something he could consider right now. There was too much left unsaid after the argument that had Lawson leaving home the second he'd graduated high school. He couldn't shake the dust off his boots from Gunner fast enough.

Working two jobs had allowed him to knock out the first two years of community college without going into debt. He'd taken out loans for his bachelor's degree, majoring in criminal justice, and had been working as a cop ever since. For the past five years, he'd worked the K9 Unit, and Kodo had been his only partner.

Kodo's ears jutted forward at the exact moment a loud thump sounded against the sliding glass doors. The noise was so loud it startled Lawson, and he was more than a little surprised the glass didn't crack or shatter on impact. His first thought was that he must have forgotten or misplaced his electric screwdriver, or a two-by-four was still out there, or the deck was splitting. But the panicked face that was pressed to the glass shocked him the most.

What on God's green earth was his former best friend's wife doing begging him to open the door?

Lawson waved Eileen inside as he made a move for the door. The commotion caused Kodo to jump into action. He sprang to attention and fired off a couple of warning barks as he made a beeline for the glass doors. He knew Eileen, so Lawson wasn't too worried about her opening the door on her own.

She slid the door open, hopped inside, and then closed it so fast he half expected there to be someone chasing her.

"What's going on?" he asked, after giving Kodo the command to stand down.

"I need a place to stay," Eileen said. The term 'doe eyes' was overused but when it came to her there wasn't a better word to describe hers. Large, honey-brown eyes stared at him, hooded by the thickest, longest lashes he'd ever seen—which was saying a lot considering his work interacting with the public had him meeting people on an almost nonstop basis. Her hair was so black that when it was dry it almost had blue streaks in it. Dripping wet, she was still one of the most beautiful women he'd ever seen. He used to joke that his best friend was lucky he'd been the one to see Eileen first that night at the honky tonk. She'd been there, so clearly out of place and her comfort zone. His buddy had said he saw her first. He threw an elbow into Lawson's ribs and said, *"I'm going to marry that woman."*

Truth be told, it was Lawson who'd made eye contact with the black-haired beauty first. For reasons he still couldn't explain, he hadn't corrected Kevin.

Eileen immediately locked the door and then flipped the light off.

"Seriously, Eileen, what the heck?" Lawson continued when she didn't immediately explain.

Her response was to hold up her right index finger as she pressed her back against the wall next to the sliding doors.

He had no idea how long they stood there. In times like these, seconds could feel like minutes as they ticked by. The only thing he knew for certain was that Eileen had better start talking soon. He owed it to his former best friend to look out for her if she was in some kind of trouble, financial or otherwise. He'd made that promise to Kevin while his friend was on his deathbed a little more than a year ago. But he hadn't been able to bring himself to check on her more than once after he realized that surge of attraction he felt when he first put eyes on her, had only grown. Seeing her so sad and so broken only made him want to bring her into his arms and hold her until the world righted itself again.

It wouldn't, though. Not for her. And in many ways not for him either. His best friend was gone and Lawson was the most horrible person in the world for coveting the man's wife. So the distance he'd kept had been to ensure that he honored his promise to Kevin, even when that meant protecting her from himself.

"What happened and who is following you?" he asked, cutting right to the chase as he stared out at the intensifying storm.

Eileen Houston was desperate. She could only hope Lawson wouldn't throw her out. The fact he'd been distant this past year—and therefore not been seen with her—made his home the last place anyone would look for her. She hoped.

"Can I stay for a little while?" she asked, figuring she might as well try. Based on his reaction to her so far, she had no idea if he would welcome her.

"Yes," Lawson said, walking over to the glass doors. "You didn't have to ask." The disappointment in his voice made her wonder how much was directed at her question or himself for not making her feel welcome. Or the fact he hadn't called to check on her after that one time in the year since Kevin's death.

"I wasn't sure where we stood," she said. Her honesty seemed to catch him off guard.

"You still haven't answered my questions." His lips thinned as the corners dipped into a frown.

She bit back the snappy comment that came to mind. "You never were one to mince words." Had it been a mistake to show up here? "You shouldn't stand there."

"I'm not the one on the run," he quipped.

She blew out a sharp breath. "I only meant to say that it's dangerous to stand in front of a window during a thunderstorm, especially with tornado sirens going off."

He shrugged. "They sound the alarm every time the wind blows these days."

Not exactly, but he wasn't too far off base. Now, they sounded the alarms to warn of severe storms too, forcing people to check their weather app or watch a meteorologist to determine whether or not they needed to hop inside their safe spot. The change was annoying.

"Hey, Kodo," Eileen said as the police dog sat at attention next to Lawson's foot. The two were never far from each other and Kodo served as a constant reminder not to get too close to his partner. She had no doubt in her mind he would snap at her if she got within a foot of Lawson. He'd already bared his teeth, a sure sign he was ready and willing to bite. Police dogs were a special breed and she had a healthy respect for them.

Lawson glanced over at her before fixing his gaze on the window. A moment later, he gave a quiet command, and Kodo immediately obeyed by standing up and then moving to his bed in the adjacent living room. He circled once, then lay down while keeping his gaze on his handler the whole time. Their bond was impressive. Police dogs were high-strung and always on alert, a requirement of the job. She remembered what Lawson had said about the early days of their partnership. He'd said it was a miracle those sharp fangs of Kodo's hadn't end up in Lawson's flesh.

Eileen didn't grow up in a house with animals. After her older sister Andrea accidently drowned at the age of eight years old while at a birthday swim party for one of their neighbors, her parents divorced. Both coped with the loss in their own way. For her father, that meant marrying one of the models who worked for him. He managed a small convention center in downtown Dallas that hosted fashion shows featuring local designers among other things. He wrapped himself up in his work and new bride, whereas Eileen's mother spiraled in another direction: sadness and anger. She had to go back to work as a schoolteacher, barely earning enough to make ends meet. Their lifestyle dropped drastically from living in a small mansion in Highland Park to moving outside the loop into a two-bedroom apartment. Her mother never dated after. She came home and sat down in front of the TV every night with a TV dinner and a glass of wine. Within a few years after Eileen moved out, her mother became sick and no matter how much Eileen tried to help, she was pushed away. The last words her mother spewed in a rage was that she only wanted to be with Andrea, which nearly shattered Eileen. She'd loved her sister too and was devastated by the loss, but always wondered why she wasn't enough for her mother to keep going. What was broken in Eileen that made her so unlovable?

After crossing his arms over a broad chest, Lawson

stepped into the kitchen area. "You haven't answered my questions."

"Because I can't," she said with a shrug. "Someone has been following me since..." She flashed eyes at him not really wanting to finish the sentence.

One of Lawson's dark eyebrows shot up. "Someone on the force?"

"No, I don't believe so. I do feel like I might have seen the face before, but I can't pinpoint where," she admitted. "Kevin's funeral?"

"Is that why you moved away so fast?" he asked. The question struck a nerve.

"That, and because I could no longer afford our house," she stated with a little more ire than intended. There was another reason that she didn't feel like getting into. She shook her head. None of this was Lawson's fault and it had probably been a mistake to show up here out of the blue. She didn't want to take her frustration out on him, and he probably didn't know anything anyway. "I'm sorry, I—"

"Don't be," he quickly countered. "If anyone should be apologizing, it's me."

"You're not the one following me and scaring me half to death," she said, confused about where he was going with this.

"No, I'm not," he agreed. "I made a promise to my best friend that I didn't keep. If you're in some kind of danger, it's my fault for not looking out for you." There was a quality to his voice that she couldn't quite pinpoint. An emotion that sounded a bit like regret and self-deprecation mixed with a whole lot of anger.

"Believe me when I say this has nothing to do with

you," she reassured. This was one of the reasons she'd hesitated in coming here in the first place, when she initially got a bad feeling about the dark-haired, military-cut person who kept showing up in odd places. When the sunglass-wearing man appeared at her job asking questions, she went into full-tilt disappear mode.

"Where did you move?" he asked.

"I'm renting a place in Bixby," she said. When he eyed her up and down, she added, "I wear this so I'll blend in with students." Her burnt orange sweatshirt and jogging pants were the perfect items to help her blend in with a student body of fifty thousand plus.

"Since when?" he asked, studying her. Was he trying to decide if he believed her? If he could trust her? If she was on some type of substance?

As awful as that sounded, she couldn't exactly blame him if he'd gone down that road. To his credit, he hadn't walked over and smelled her breath or checked her pupils. Maybe she was being dramatic in her assessment but surviving the year since losing Kevin after being married less than twelve months had set her on edge.

They hadn't even made it out of the honeymoon stage before he was gone. She knew the risks in marrying a cop, at least on an academic level. He'd reassured her time and time again that he would come home every night.

Losing him had ranked right up there with one of the worst days of her life. Finding out that he might have been working for the wrong side of the law had shattered everything she believed she knew about the man. For a split second, she wondered if Lawson had known about Kevin's other dealings. She told herself that coming here and talking to him would prove that Lawson was innocent.

Was that the real reason she'd shown up? A little voice in the back of her mind said the fact she needed to see him came from somewhere else, some place she couldn't allow herself to go mentally.

"How well did you know Kevin?" she asked the man who'd been her husband's best friend.

CHAPTER TWO

Eileen's question threw Lawson for a loop. "He was my best friend." He shrugged. "I guess I knew him better than most. Why?"

"Someone just almost ran me off the road. If another vehicle hadn't come along at the right moment, I'm not sure what might have happened." Her gaze widened. "I've seen the person before."

"Tires slip on wet roads. Are you certain about—"

"He's been watching me, Lawson. And I'm not sure what's going on." She threw her hands in the air. "I came across a few personal items in Kevin's belongings a few weeks ago and I started asking questions. I made a phone call. Now, I suddenly have a tail and I'm not sure what's going on, but I'm scared."

"Then, you're welcome to stay here while we figure it out together." Lawson made the offer with the full knowledge having her under the same roof would not make his life any easier. "I need to make a phone call first."

She cocked her head to one side and drew her eyebrows together in confusion.

"I'm supposed to head back to Gunner tomorrow morning," he explained. "There is something going on with my dad's health."

"Then you can't stay here with me. You have to go." Eileen was already shaking her head before he'd finished his sentence. "I'll figure something else out."

"I gave my word to Kevin and let him down once. Two times isn't an option," he said with finality. "Besides, my entire family is going home. All four of my brothers along with my seven cousins will be there for my father. They can keep me posted via cell phone if he takes a turn."

"No. I can't let you do that," she argued.

He fished his cell out of his pocket and held it in the air. "Times like these are what mobile phones were invented for."

"The guy who is following me hasn't technically done anything yet," she said. "What if this is all just my imagination working overtime? It could turn out to be nothing and then you might miss out on something big with your family. I can't be the reason you're not home for a family event involving your dad's health."

"How long will that last?" he asked. "How long before the guy acts again? What then?" She didn't come here of all places in a panic just to decide there was no real threat. She wouldn't have shown up if there'd been another place to go. He'd seen it on her face and in the desperation in her eyes.

"I'll figure it out." She twisted her fingers together like she did when she was nervous.

"Alone?"

The word seemed to strike a nerve when her face pinched like someone had sucked all the air out of the room and she was trying to hold onto the last bit of oxygen left in her lungs. Well, hell, he hadn't intended to hurt her feelings or remind her of the fact she had no one else to lean on, or she wouldn't be standing in his home.

A crack of thunder split the air, causing her to jump. She immediately pressed her hand to her chest as though trying to calm a racing heart.

"Hey, look, I didn't mean to—"

She waved him off before he could finish his sentence. "I know."

"Despite my poor manners up to now, it's good to see you again," he said, not wanting to admit just how far the statement went. "Have you eaten dinner yet?"

"No, but I should probably go." She headed toward the sliding glass door, stopping only when a show of lightning lit up the black sky.

"Hold on. The least I can do is feed you before you head out. I have another beer too." He motioned first toward the bottle on the table, thinking there was no way he would let her leave and drive in a storm beer or not.

"A beer would be nice," she said after a long pause. She held out her hand and showed how much it trembled along with a half-smile. "Caffeine would only make this worse."

"Beer it is." He immediately moved to the fridge before she changed her mind. "I can't promise much in the food department. There isn't much more than a sandwich and chips around here."

"Those sound good to me." She seemed to force a wider smile even though her eyes told a different story. Fear. Regret? The first was a no-brainer, but the second might just be him seeing something he wanted to.

Since acting on an attraction to Eileen was out of the question now and always, he gave himself a mental headshake and moved to the kitchen.

Putting together a sandwich didn't take long. Neither did grabbing and opening a beer. By the time he finished, she sat at the kitchen table and had positioned her handbag on the back of the chair. Kodo snored from the next room. They'd had a long, exhausting shift and Kodo had earned every minute of sleep. It was also a good sign that he trusted Eileen. Or, at the very least, had decided she wasn't a threat. So much about his and Kodo's relationship was about reading each other. A handler and canine partner became very good at picking up on signs the other was tense or relaxed. The connection was unlike anything Lawson had experienced. He trusted Kodo implicitly and vice versa. Kodo obeyed Lawson's commands despite the fact he would snap at another person in a second. He was trained to chase and stop an offender. The way it was done was by launching at the person running and then attacking until called off.

No one wanted to be on the wrong end of those incisors.

"I read somewhere police dogs follow the scent of fear when they're chasing after someone," Eileen said as he put a plate down in front of her loaded with a sandwich and chips. He set the cold beer down next as she looked up at him. "Is that true?"

He nodded. "Yes. Kodo goes after the scent of adrenaline that comes as a byproduct of fear. Once he locks onto someone's scent, it's game on."

"Interesting." She rocked her head before taking a bite.

Lawson took a sip of beer as the thunder rolled in the background. "He almost washed out of training over the sound of thunder." He nodded toward Kodo. "Look at him now. Fast asleep like he doesn't have a care in the world."

"Busy shift?" she asked in between bites.

He nodded. "I can't think of a place he'd rather be than on the job though. He's the first one ready and eager to head off for work. I've been wondering how he would handle himself at the family ranch."

Her eyebrows drew together again while she chewed.

"You know my family owns a cattle ranch, right?" He couldn't imagine she wasn't in the loop. Though, to be fair, he never talked about his past, not even with Kevin. They joked around and teased each other a whole lot. They teamed up on the basketball court during police versus firefighter events and crushed the competition if he did say so himself. They were buddies who did things together and those 'things' didn't involve talking about their pasts or their feelings for that matter. They met up at each other's homes to watch football games when their days off matched up. There were a couple of outdoor bars that allowed animals. Lawson didn't go anywhere without Kodo. If a place didn't allow his canine partner inside, it wasn't good enough for Lawson. Period.

Once Kevin married Eileen, Lawson had lost his best friend. Another reason marriage wasn't for him. Lawson liked his life just fine the way it was. He didn't need someone else to complete him. He was a whole human being already.

Eileen figured she might as well get to the point. Lawson deserved to know what he was dealing with before she agreed to accept his help. The problem was that she didn't even know.

"I already mentioned someone is watching and following me," she started, hoping the words would come to her as lightning lit up the night sky.

"How long has this been going on?"

"About a month as far as I know, maybe more if he was being stealthy about it. I thought I saw him at the funeral but decided I was losing my mind. That whole time period is such a blur." The thought made her skin crawl.

"What does this have to do with Kevin?" He took a long pull of beer and then rolled the beveled edge around his fingers before setting it down on the solid wood table. She had to suppress the urge to locate a coaster and slip it underneath the bottle to protect the beautiful oak.

She sighed because going into this was going to stir up a hornet's nest if she was wrong. "As far as Kevin's death goes..."

The muscles in Lawson's jaw ticked.

"What if his death wasn't in the line of duty?"

Lawson shook his head. "Kevin died a hero."

"He was shot while on duty," she said, choosing her words carefully.

"How is that any different than what I just said?" he asked, accusation in his tone. The two had been inseparable before the wedding, according to Kevin. So much so, he expected some tension after she and Kevin returned from their honeymoon. Kevin became so wrapped up in moving into their new home, painting, and fixing it up that he worried Lawson would become jealous and their friendship would take a hit. Lawson refused multiple invitations to come over and watch football as they settled in. Each time, he seemed to come up with a different excuse. When Kevin called his friend out, Lawson told him to stop worrying and enjoy time with his new bride. The more his best friend withdrew, the deeper Kevin's concern became. Eileen figured it out before Kevin. His best friend didn't like her. She had no idea why.

"Kevin may have been shot for personal reasons," she finally said. "He just happened to be on the job when the shooting occurred."

"Who else have you told this to?" Lawson's forehead wrinkled with concern. His welcoming reaction to her showing up unannounced without wanting to give reasons right away made her wonder if she'd pegged him all wrong after the wedding. Maybe he really *had* been just giving her and Kevin space to get to know each other as husband and wife.

"No one," she said. "Why?"

"Because this news could cause an internal investigation to open, and you could lose all your benefits if what you're saying is true." He held up a hand. "I'm not saying it is or isn't. This isn't me judging you. I'm being practical."

"It isn't right for me to keep the pension or have everyone's sympathy if he was dirty, Lawson."

Those words seemed to strike like physical blows to the chest. He took a few seconds to process the information. This was news to him based on his reaction. And yet there was something going on across his features that said he might be reevaluating information or exchanges the two had had.

"My best friend died a hero," Lawson repeated a little too emphatically, like he was trying to convince himself too.

"That's what I want to believe," she reassured. "In fact, I'd like nothing more than to be one hundred percent wrong about this, about him. We were married for heaven's sake. I loved him." She'd been swept away by the handsome lawman who was so full of charm when he'd approached her—saved her was more like it—from the date she'd been on. The first man she'd seen that night who released a dozen butterflies in her chest had been Lawson, but it had been Kevin who approached her. She assumed Lawson wasn't attracted to her, despite the crackle of electricity she felt the second their eyes connected from across the room. Their energy went from fire to freezer so fast it almost made her head spin. So much so, she'd convinced herself that she had to have been the only one who'd felt their chemistry.

"Let's circle back to the beginning. Tell me why you think Kevin might have been dirty and how that might be connected to what is going on with you right now," he said in his more authoritative investigator tone. She recognized the change instantly. It seemed like all law enforcement officers had two distinct voices. The one they used in everyday life and the one that let the world know they were cops. Kevin had explained the reason for the duality. He had to be able to walk into any situation and take control. It started with confidence in his tone. Plus, when folks were in a panic, they usually listened to the person who sounded like they were in charge.

"A few months into our marriage I started to suspect he might be cheating," she admitted, bringing her gaze down to the rim of her beer.

"No way." Lawson spoke the words with confidence she didn't feel.

"You asked me to go back to the beginning and essentially tell you everything," she pointed out.

"Fair enough," he said. Lawson's deep baritone sounded like whiskey being poured over ice. It had a way of moving over her skin that made her suddenly aware of a male presence in the room despite how much she tried to fight her reaction to him.

"There were calls taken in the garage after I'd gone to bed." The fears she'd made a mistake in marrying Kevin twisted her stomach as much now as they had then. "When I asked him about them, he seemed surprised I knew. But he had an excuse for them. He said they were work calls and needed to be taken in private."

Lawson blew out a frustrated-sounding breath. "If you believe that, I have a bridge for sale." His words came out incredulous, and another emotion she couldn't quite pinpoint.

She shot him a look that must've resonated because he put his hand up again, palm out.

"Sorry," he said. "I do realize you're not that naïve. I meant it more as a general statement, but it didn't come across the right way. You're too intelligent to believe a line like that one."

"It's fine." She didn't want to admit how much the off-handed remark stung coming from Lawson. "The point is that he was lying to me. My mind immediately snapped to an affair."

"Understandable, but I happen to know Kevin was crazy about you," he said with a note in his tone that she picked up on but couldn't quite figure out. Her brain automatically snapped to jealousy but that was impossible. She'd made eye contact with Lawson first that night and he'd taken a pass on speaking to her first. He'd willingly stepped aside and allowed his friend to ask her out.

"Doesn't mean he wouldn't cheat," she stated. "After my sister died..." She flashed eyes at him, realizing he probably had no idea about her past.

"I'm sorry for your loss." His words came out as though on autopilot, like he'd probably said that dozens of times to civilians in the line of duty. And yet there was so much sincerity in his tone that she believed he meant it.

"It was a long time ago," she said by way of explanation. "But thank you. It means a lot."

"And you're not off base about the cheating accusation," he continued. "I've seen it with other officers. I just didn't think of Kevin being in the same boat as some of the others." He clenched his jaw muscles as though saying those words brought out anger he couldn't afford to unleash and had to clamp down on.

"He was your best friend until I came along," she pointed out.

"True," he said.

"He talked about how much honor and loyalty you had." Kevin talked about Lawson as though he was a saint. "Said you were in a class by yourself, and he respected the hell out of you for it."

"I thought we held the same beliefs," he admitted with another look of apology. She didn't want him to look at her that way, with pity. On a primal level, she wanted more from Lawson even though nothing could ever happen between them.

CHAPTER THREE

Consider Lawson's mind blown. There was no way he could imagine his best friend having an affair. He also wanted to circle back and ask about what happened to Eileen's sister, despite the warning going off in the back of his mind about getting too close. Being objective meant keeping a safe distance from Eileen. And he needed to stay neutral if he was to keep Eileen safe.

"Tell me more about the possible affair," he said, not really able to go there without proof, even though her instincts were pointing otherwise, and he knew full well a woman's intuition was right more often than wrong.

"That's what I thought early in our marriage, but before I could confirm anything..." She snapped her fingers and shook her head. "He was gone. By then, it didn't seem worth trying to follow up on my suspicions. What would it prove?"

"Did you see anyone at the funeral who might have been mourning more than others? Crying a little too hard? Dressed differently? Maybe like she'd just lost her spouse?" he asked. If he was in the situation, he would want to know the truth no matter how much it would gut him if his wife was having an affair.

"I scanned every single face for the signs you just mentioned," she admitted on a shrug. "Saw nothing that screamed anyone had been his mistress but then I wouldn't have known what to look for anyway." She paused for a couple of beats. "I'm not proud of the fact, but I went through his pockets after the funeral looking for something. Anything. I'm not sure what I thought I would find. A love letter? Who handwrites notes any longer since phones came along?"

"Not me and I'm not exactly the biggest fan of technology when I'm off the job," he admitted.

"Shouldn't there be some scrap of paper somewhere though? Some kind of evidence? He was too smart to use text because I sometimes brought his cell phone to him if he was in the next room when it rang." She paused another beat before continuing. "Frustrated and just plain sad, I sort of forced myself to look the other way and box up Kevin's personal effects. I moved into the new place without giving it another thought." She flashed her eyes at him and he instantly knew she wasn't telling him something important. "I chose to move on and believe he was faithful in the marriage. I've spent the past twelve months trying to figure out how to live my life as a widow."

Those were heavy words, so he didn't try to fill the air with meaningless chatter. All he could do at this point was nod. He couldn't imagine falling in love and then losing the person almost as quickly as he'd found them.

"What about online?" he finally asked. "Wouldn't there be e-mails or direct messages on social media accounts?"

"Probably but I'd just lost my husband and wasn't in my right mind," she admitted. There was something behind her eyes that he couldn't put his finger on. Lawson was good at his job. He was even better at spotting someone covering the truth or flat-out lying. Eileen didn't strike him as a liar, so what was she covering?

"About a month and a half ago, I decided to go through the boxes one by one to see what I wanted to keep for..."

There she went with those eyes again. She quickly recovered.

"For memory's sake," she continued. "I finally found a scrap of paper. I didn't have the heart to get rid of any of Kevin's belongings at first, so when I boxed everything up, it all went inside sight unseen. This scrap had a number on it in his handwriting. I immediately thought I was right about the affair. I called the number ready to hear the voice of the woman my husband chose over our marriage."

"I'm guessing it didn't go down that way," he surmised.

"Not in the least," she continued. "Someone answered but I have no idea who because they didn't speak. All I heard was breathing and what sounded like a train in the background. I'm guessing the person on the other end of the line was waiting for me to go. Instead of saying a word, I panicked and ended the call." She bit down on her bottom lip. "If that was an affair, wouldn't she have said something?"

"I'd hate to base an accusation of that weight on the exchange you just described," he stated.

"Right. But then, this guy with a military haircut, who is always positioned so I can't see his face, suddenly appears wherever I am," she explained. "Her husband?"

"That part is not just creepy, it's cause for concern," he admitted. "Has this person approached you in any way?" His mind was already thinking like a cop. He wanted to figure it out and get a restraining order on the guy at the very least.

"It's not like that," she said. "A couple of days later, I'm one hundred percent certain that someone was in my house while I was at work."

"You're thinking it might have been the person from the call?" he asked, figuring he already knew how she would answer. A good investigator asked every question, even the ones he believed he had answers to.

"I believe so, but I can't prove anything," she said.

"Was anything missing? Or did you notice a broken window? How did the perp get inside your place?" he continued, realizing he was firing questions faster than she could reasonably answer. He didn't stop himself though until he asked one more. "And, more importantly, did you call the law about the break-in?"

She shook her head. "Honestly, I had this fear that I'd somehow imagined the whole thing. It took me a couple of days to sort through my emotions." Her timelines bothered him and he couldn't pinpoint the reason. Not yet anyway. "So, no, I didn't call the law." She made a tsk sound. "What would they have done anyway?"

Her point was valid. There wasn't much they could do without a real crime scene or proof a crime had occurred. The police had to have evidence to go by, not suspicion, which seemed to be all she had so far.

"Where is that?" he asked. "Your workplace?"

"I've been working at a plant nursery," she said. "Trying to put my biology degree to work in a feat that hasn't exactly been easy."

"Wouldn't that qualify you to work in a lab?" he asked.

"Yes, at about ten dollars an hour under horrid conditions," she said on what sounded like a frustrated sigh. "I should have looked ahead to what kind of job I would have after getting a degree but, honestly, I was just so happy to be away from my family after my sister's death that I would have majored in basket weaving to leave home. Being around plants always calmed me down and made me feel like I could really breathe again."

He nodded. Being home on the ranch with fields that seemed to go on forever and a sky that did the same had always centered him.

"Do you mind if I asked what happened to your sister?" He might regret asking the question, but this was the second time she'd mentioned her family and the loss.

"My older sister drowned at a neighbor's swimming pool when we were just kids," she said. "I was six years old and she was eight."

"I'm sorry," he stated. "I can't even imagine what that must have been like, but a child's death is the most unnatural thing, in my opinion."

"I couldn't agree more," she said. "Andrea's death broke my parents. I didn't really understand how that might happen when I was younger. I guess I was selfish in wanting them to feel like they still had me and that I could somehow fill the hole in their chests." She shrugged. "But they loved her very much, and the accident tore my parents apart. Their marriage crumbled. My dad cheated." Again, she looked up at him causing a bomb to detonate in his chest. He ignored it. "I'm not certain what came first to be honest."

"What about you?" he asked.

"I don't ever remember anyone asking me that question," she said with a surprised look on her face. "My parents pulled me out of school for the rest of the year as the accident happened in late May. I'm sure they believed they were doing what was best for me. Or maybe they were just too broken to do basic things, like get me to school on time."

"The loss combined with a break in routine must have been difficult for a child to process. All the training I've received says keeping a routine can be a huge help in times of trauma." He couldn't fathom losing one of his brothers or cousins at such a young age. Hell, the family had been through more than any should in recent months and he'd been worried beyond belief. Thankfully, every last one was still standing. The incidents were reminders of how important family was to him. As soon as he made good on his promise to protect Eileen, he intended to head home to be there for his father. Guilt was a gut punch when it came to his relationship with Archer Quinn. It would only get worse if he didn't find a way to make peace with his father.

All the more reason to get to the bottom of who was

following Eileen and put her mind at ease. "Do you mind if I take a look at Kevin's personal effects?"

"I guess that would be all right." Eileen was thrown for a loop with the question. When she took a second to reason it out, it made sense. Lawson was an investigator. He worked in law enforcement. He would know what to look for.

"Has the guy with the military cut been seen outside your home?"

"As a matter of fact, I'm almost certain he was the one who followed me there from work one day. I got this weird feeling but decided that I was being paranoid," she remembered.

"Can I give you a word of advice?" he asked.

She nodded.

"Always listen to your gut. If it's wrong, no harm has been done. On the other hand..."

"If it's right," she continued for him, "I wouldn't be in this situation right now. At least, no one would know where I moved to."

"Anyone who is persistent can find you now," he immediately said.

"Are you trying to make me feel better for the mistake?" she asked.

"Would it work?"

"I might be willing to buy it, considering I've beat myself up over what I could have missed," she admitted. The rain had calmed down, turning into more of a light sprinkle now.

"Don't," he said, "it's a waste of energy." The confidence in his statement almost made her believe it too. She wanted to believe she hadn't brought any of this on herself because everything had been quiet before she made that phone call. "I'm sorry you didn't feel like you had enough support here to stick around or tell anyone about the move. You would have had more volunteers to help you than you could have handled. If I'd known, I would have—"

"It's not your fault," she quickly countered, cutting in before he could get too far down the familiar path of self-blame.

"I'm the one he asked to watch out for you," he said, and then he smacked his flat palm against the oak hard enough to wake Kodo. The dog jumped to attention, so Lawson quietly gave the command to sit. Kodo shook like he'd just come out of a bath. Then, he obeyed. "It's possible that he knew someone might come for you."

Lawson had been right beside Kevin in the hospital moments before his friend had taken his last breath. Why didn't Kevin issue a warning?

"Those were his last words to me," he continued. "I thought he meant in the general sense but he didn't. He specifically asked me to take care of you in your vulnerable..."

His eyes sparked. His gaze dropped as though he could see through the wood to her stomach. He'd figured it out.

"Condition," he said, finished his sentence.

"We were two months pregnant when Kevin was killed," she explained. "Too early to show or tell anyone.

The doctor said wait until three months once we could be certain the pregnancy would be viable."

"And?"

"I had a boy and named him Kevin," she admitted. "He's four months old now."

"Where is he now?" he asked.

"With a neighbor. Millie Davis is retired, and her husband passed away a few years ago," she explained. "She said watching Kevin has given her purpose again. She wasn't able to conceive, so she started a different kind of nursery. She's the one who gave me a job when I showed up in Bixby a widower with a baby on the way. She owns the place where I work. Said she couldn't bear to sell the business after her husband passed away because it had always been their baby. But she also doesn't have the wherewithal to keep up with the demands, either."

And then it dawned on her the person who'd followed her home could try something with her neighbor. She gasped. "You don't think Millie is in any sort of danger because of me, do you?"

"I don't think so based on what you've told me so far," he reassured. "You called a number and now someone is watching you. Someone may have broken into your home but they slipped in and out, so they didn't want you to realize they were there. There are a couple of possibilities here as to why that would be. The person on the other end of the line might believe you know something and is watching to see what you plan to do with the information. Or Kevin possessed something either of value or that might incriminate someone."

"That means he was involved in illegal activity," she stated.

"It's possible, no matter how much I don't want to believe it could be," he said, before picking up his beer bottle by the rim between two fingers and his thumb. He took a swig before placing it back down on the oak.

"Is it awful to prefer my husband was involved in criminal activity, as opposed to having an affair?"

"Not in my book," he said. "I'm still holding out hope neither one is true." His lips compressed into a frown before the spark returned to his eyes. "I can access the report to see if there are any inconsistencies or red flags on the line-of-duty shooting. Despite an internal review, something might have been missed. Especially if no one suspected Kevin of foul play or wrongdoing."

"The possibility caught you off guard and you were his best friend," she said. "It stands to reason that he was able to cover up his dealings well enough to get past the people he cared about the most."

"Had your bank account received an infusion of funds during that time or in the months before his death?" he asked.

"No." She shook her head.

"Doesn't mean there isn't an account that you don't know about, sitting out there with money in it," he reasoned. "Maybe we can find something in Kevin's belongings."

"I saved his personal laptop." She'd kept it for nostalgia considering she had her own. "It's password protected, though I have no clue what the password might be."

"We can always take it to a guru and get information." His lips formed a grim line. "For now, I'd like to keep our suspicions between us and not bring in the department."

"I'd like to maintain Kevin's reputation as well," she said, thinking how much this news might affect her son in the years to come. Nothing was ever private anymore. If she could hold onto this and give her son a memory of his father that was good, she wanted to try. "At some point, I do realize the law might have to be involved." She issued a sharp sigh. "I want my son to know who his father was, but I'd like to protect him from vultures if at all possible. Don't get me wrong, if Kevin broke the law, he doesn't deserve hero status. But I've seen situations blow up and families run out of town when they had nothing to do with the crimes. Bixby is still close enough to Austin for people to find us."

"We'll be as sensitive about this as we can," he promised. It was a promise she hoped he could keep.

"The rain seems to have slowed down. When do you want to go through Kevin's things?" she asked.

"Now is good for me."

Eileen took in a slow breath and nodded. She finished the last sip of beer and then said, "I'm as ready as I'll ever be to find out my husband might have been a criminal."

CHAPTER FOUR

Lawson would do everything in his power to make good on his promise to Eileen. He glanced over at Kodo, who'd settled down, and decided to let him stay home. Besides, they needed to be as stealth as possible so as not to raise any alarms to their presence.

"How long can Millie keep the baby?" he asked Eileen as they exited his home. The thought of Eileen having a child shouldn't be the gut punch that it turned out to be. She'd been married to Kevin. It was only natural they would talk about starting a family. He couldn't help but wonder why they'd rushed into it. Kevin had kept quiet about the baby. He'd joked about not being fatherhood material. Had meeting 'the one' changed those views? Lawson had seen it happen within his family, and yet he couldn't ignore his instincts that said Kevin would have taken the pregnancy news hard.

"Overnight at a minimum. More if needed," she said. "He can't end up collateral damage in this, Lawson. He's innocent and doesn't deserve any of this."

"I couldn't agree more," he said before adding, "and neither do you."

As he locked up, Kodo appeared at the glass, nervous. He paced back and forth. His ears were forward and it looked as though a concern line wrinkled his forehead. Lawson glanced over at Eileen. "I'd thought about leaving him here, but do you mind if he tags along? He isn't usually like this and must have picked up on the tension between us." There had been a lot of crackling energy in the room and Kodo must have noticed that too. It seemed to make him uncomfortable. At the very least, he was aware. This shouldn't surprise Lawson in the least, considering the two of them were constant companions and experts at reading each other's body language. The trouble was that Lawson had brought dates home and once the initial greeting took place, Kodo didn't give any of the others the time of day.

"I don't mind at all," Eileen said. "In fact, it's reassuring to have him around even though I'm one hundred percent certain he doesn't like me one bit."

"What makes you say that?" Lawson opened the door. Kodo went straight to Lawson's side.

"The look on his face, for one. The fact he doesn't come up to me and sniff, for another," she said.

"I'll give you the no-sniff comment, but that's only because he doesn't do that to anyone," he defended. "The look on his face is pretty much how he looks all the time. It's a cross between grumpy old man and concern."

"Those eyes, though," she said as they walked toward his Jeep. "They're so deep and expressive. And they definitely aren't friendly toward me no matter how beautiful they are."

"The fact he hasn't growled at you once, since showing up at the door unexpectedly, is a sign he actually might like you," he explained as he opened the door for her and Kodo. His dog jumped in first and she seemed content to wait for him to clear the front seat before climbing in behind him.

"This is okay, right?" she asked, before he closed the door.

"You're doing fine with him," Lawson reassured before moving around the front of the vehicle and then taking the driver's seat. He scanned the area looking for her vehicle. "Where are you parked?"

"A couple blocks away," she said. "Practically in a ditch. I panicked when the other vehicle swerved into my lane right in front of me. I'm surprised we didn't crash to tell you the truth. My tires sank into the mud on the side of the road. When I looked up, I realized how close I was to your place."

"Come to think of it, how do you know where I live?" he asked, realizing she'd never been to his home before.

She smacked the flat of her palm against her knee. "You know, I didn't think about how odd this was until now. One day, Kevin and I were driving to a cabin for the weekend and he said that he was taking the long way around to point out where you lived. I didn't think much about it at the time because we weren't in a hurry. There was a lot of traffic on the main road that day, so I just assumed he wanted to avoid it by going around."

"Seems like he might have suspected you might

need to find me someday," he surmised. He didn't like where any of this was going. It meant his close friend might have been a dirty cop, which was something he despised. The job was difficult enough, without his own kind making it harder on the good guys. A large part of him didn't want to put Kevin in the other category. If he'd done something illegal, Lawson wanted there to be a rational explanation for the actions.

"I abandoned my car down the street and ran in the opposite direction before circling back in case the person following me knew your address too," she admitted. The thought didn't sit well but it was possible. She was also thinking like a good investigator.

"Smart," was all he said as he started the engine. "Where are we headed?"

"Bixby," she said, before she seemed to realize he wasn't familiar with the town. "It's just shy of an hour from here. It's one of those small towns outside of Austin that if you blink, you'll miss it."

She gave him the quick and dirty directions as he nodded. He was familiar with the area, if not the actual town. There were plenty of small towns in these parts, each with their own personality.

"How much does Kevin's family know?" he asked, remembering his buddy had a sister who lived in Louisiana. They'd rarely talked about Kevin's folks. When the subject came up, Kevin moved on quickly.

"His parents asked me to let them have the baby," she said, much to his shock. "I went to them after the doctor gave me the green light to share the news. When I showed up to their home, they treated me fine even though they didn't seem all that happy to see me at first."

"What changed their minds?" he asked.

"When they found out I was pregnant," she said. "For a minute there, I thought they might actually try to fight for custody. Kevin wasn't exactly close with his parents but losing him had to have been hard on them. Well, his mother anyway. I didn't get the impression his stepfather was terribly sad about the news. He seemed to take it in stride, shrugging his shoulders and mumbling something about life being cruel before grabbing the TV remote and 'leaving us women' to talk."

"His mother's pain was no excuse to try to take your child," he quipped, thinking he didn't like Kevin's stepfather all that much. "You were hurting too."

"True," she said with a nod as he navigated onto the highway, heading southwest. "His mother backed off when his sister stepped in. She reminded both of them that they probably didn't want to upset the mother of their grandchild."

"I don't remember Kevin mentioning that he even had a sister."

"Did you guys sit around and talk or watch football games together and then go shoot hoops?" she asked after a thoughtful pause.

"We spoke, though we didn't exactly braid each other's hair, if that's what you're insinuating," he defended. From the corner of his eye, he could see her crack a smile.

"You know what I mean," she said.

"I do," he conceded. "And I was trying to be funny."

"Well, it worked," she said. Was it wrong that he

liked the fact he was able to lighten her load even a little bit? Humor was the way most officers diffused tension, and it was nice to see her smile again, even if it wouldn't last.

"It appears that I didn't know as much about his personal life as I should have, considering he was my best friend." The two of them had watched games, shot hoops, and gone out to a honky tonk bar on occasion. They'd been each other's wingman. They'd gone down to 5th Street to listen to new and favorite bands. Should Lawson consider it odd that he didn't know much about Kevin's family, except they lived in Louisiana?

"He told me that you were from a big and famous cattle ranching family," she offered. If that was supposed to make him feel better, it didn't work. He was beginning to realize he didn't know Kevin as well as he'd once believed. And that knowledge opened a can of worms as far as he was concerned. How well had Lawson known his best friend if he didn't even know the man had a sister?

"Seems one of us knew the other," he said on a sigh.

"She's his half-sister if that helps," Eileen added, as though that might make this better. "She's ten years younger than him. Same mother, different dads."

"It still would have been nice for this to come up once in the three years we hung out," he said, hearing the tinge of hurt in his own voice.

"For what it's worth, I think he was embarrassed."

Her comment threw Lawson for a loop.

"About having a half-sister?" he asked.

She shook her head. "His family in general. They

don't have a lot of money and live in small parish in Louisiana. Kevin looked up to you in a way."

Lawson put his hand up to stop her right there. "Don't tell me that. We were friends. Equals."

"Not in his book, you weren't," she said.

Those words stung. How could he have been so far off base with someone he considered his best friend? And why did people feel the need to keep secrets? Lawson wasn't the kind of person who would judge someone else based on the size of their bank account. If anyone pegged him as someone who would care about that over being a good person, they didn't know what ranchers were made of.

"What made me so different from everyone else?" Lawson asked with a hint of hurt in his tone. He covered it, but Eileen had picked up on it. Was coming from a family of financial means an embarrassment to him?

"He looked up to you more than he probably ever let you know," Eileen said. Spending even a little time with Lawson made it easy to see why Kevin would admire his friend. "Like a big brother."

"We were the same age," he countered.

"You know what I mean." She wasn't finding the right words but he had to get the gist of what she was saying.

He got quiet for a long moment as the windshield wipers swished back and forth. The methodical rhythm was strangely comforting. Or maybe it was being here with Lawson. He was tall and had a physical presence bigger than any room. To someone on the wrong side of the law, his size was probably intimidating, but for her, he felt solid. Reassuring.

Lawson had the kind of quiet confidence that said he could handle himself in pretty much any situation that came his way. Kevin hadn't been as sure of himself, especially in the last month or two before his death. Had a problem been building? Something he couldn't talk about with her? Or his best friend?

It shouldn't surprise her that he wouldn't want to admit anything to Lawson given how much Kevin looked up to his friend. Lawson was the first person Kevin mentioned to her when he started coming home late. He left early for work, saying he wanted to get in some overtime since they'd just bought a small house on the outskirts of Austin. Kevin hadn't been ready to start a family right away. She'd wanted to spend a little more time getting to know each other. Their romance had been a whirlwind. She'd fallen fast and hard for Kevin, believing that what they had was the best it would ever get.

No one had made her feel as special as him. No one had come close to stirring up feelings deep in her chest before him. No one had gotten her to agree to a date or marriage proposal as quickly.

Only now, with the way her heart pounded the inside of her ribs when Lawson was near, did she realize there could have been even more.

Shoving the thought aside, she forced her thoughts back on the conversation thread from a minute ago.

"I'm just trying to relay how much Kevin respected you. I wasn't trying to offend you in any way."

Lawson nodded. "Is it strange that I called him my best friend and was oblivious to all of it?" he asked, tightening his grip on the steering wheel. His gaze was intent on the stretch of road in front of them as the rain decreased to not much more than a drizzle.

"People only show the side of themselves they want others to see," she said with a shrug. The statement was truer than she wanted it to be and applied to her as well as Lawson. "He would have been too embarrassed to actually tell you any of it anyway."

"I guess we didn't exactly share our feelings," he said. "And I didn't realize how much I must keep everyone at arm's length until this conversation. I was perfectly fine with our friendship right where it was. I didn't need to know more about his family or how he grew up. My family, my life is public knowledge and I forget that too. Quinns make headlines whether we want to or not. It's been that way my entire life, so I tend to shove the knowledge under the rug."

"Is that why you work in law enforcement and not on the ranch?" she asked before realizing she might be overstepping her bounds. "You don't have to answer that if you don't want to."

"No, it's fine," he countered. "Yes, in a way it is. My uncle is the one who made a fortune in the cattle ranching business. My father worked in law enforcement."

"You followed in his footsteps then," she surmised, a little surprised when his jaw muscle ticked like she'd just stepped on a landmine.

"I guess so," was all he said by way of response, and she could sense there was a whole lot more to the story. She wouldn't push, though. He was helping her and she didn't want to offend him.

Then, Lawson issued a sharp sigh.

"My brothers and I went into law enforcement as a family identity of sorts," he explained. "Our cousins were cattle ranchers and, I guess, we figured we needed an identity. Since law enforcement was all we knew from our father, we headed down the same path. My brother Griff is the oldest and he is a sheriff. Harding and Barrett are U.S. Marshals. Crawford works for Austin PD, or did until recently. I haven't spoken to him about his career change yet, but I've heard rumor he is moving back to Quinnland to work the land."

"Seems like a drastic change," she said and then her mouth formed an O. "He's the officer who had a bomb strapped to his chest in a standoff with the dangerous escaped convict, isn't he?"

Lawson nodded. "Thankfully, he came out in one piece."

"That had to be horrific for him and the whole family," she said. "I read an article about the incident, if it can be called that. 'Incident' seems too small of a word. Ordeal?"

"It was that and so much more."

"I can only imagine." Eileen was so young when her sister died the memories weren't fresh. The pain was still there even if the details had been erased from her thoughts, most likely because her young brain had gone into survival mode. All she had left were the residual feelings and a few glimpses; her sister in a casket, her parents sobbing, and the fight between the two people she loved that changed all three of their lives forever. Living it now as an adult must have been terrifying for the family. "According to the article, it turned out okay. I'm sure it wasn't that simple."

"No, but we're handling it," he said in a rare show of vulnerability.

"Is that why your brother is leaving law enforcement?" she asked.

"I intended to find that out when I went home tomorrow, but plans have changed," he said.

"On my account," she said low and under her breath.

"Not your fault," he said. "So don't blame yourself. You didn't ask for any of this in your life and you sure as heck don't deserve it. Neither you nor Kevin Jr. do. I'm just glad you made the decision to come to me before it got too out of hand and something truly tragic happened. Right now, we can fix this."

I hope so, she thought even though she didn't see the way.

CHAPTER FIVE

Conversation ended a moment before Lawson turned onto Eileen's cul-de-sac. The homes in this area had no sidewalks or signs of city life. The yards in similar places he'd visited were usually an acre at a minimum. He couldn't quite get his bearings in the dark to figure out what the landscape actually looked like. His headlights illuminated the stretch of road in front of them. Houses were set back from the road. A town this small most likely didn't have individual mailboxes at homes to check for a street number. Then again, he didn't need it while Eileen was beside him.

"Which house is Millie's?" he asked, figuring he needed to get the lay of the land.

"The one we just passed on the right," she said, turning her head and pointing.

"How many homes are on this street?" he continued, making a mental map.

"Three," she informed. "Millie's, mine, and Cary's."

"Do you know who Cary is?" he asked, his radar going up.

"He's a retiree," she stated. "His wife recently passed away and his kids are trying to get him to move to Dallas to be near them and the grandchildren."

That seemed to be how it usually worked with families. When both grandparents were alive, the kids figured all was well. The day that number changed, folks started to worry. Part of his job before moving to the canine unit had him doing wellness checks on elderly Austin residents. It was true. No one should live alone. He considered the irony in that statement, considering he never pictured himself settling down. Maybe someday he would consider it *if* the right person came along when he was ready to take a big step like that one. He worried about his brothers and their relationships. What was their rush to get engaged?

A little voice in the back of his mind picked that moment to point out the fact his cousins had been through similar seemingly whirlwind romances, and they were all doing just fine. His brothers wouldn't take a subject like marriage lightly. Why did they feel the need to lock in after only knowing someone for days or weeks?

When you know, you know. Was that statement true? If he'd talked to Eileen first instead of Kevin, how different would all of their lives be now?

Speaking of his friend, Lawson was still reeling over the information from the car ride. He'd considered Kevin an equal in every sense of the word. To say the news Kevin didn't see the friendship the same way was a shock, was a whole lot like saying bees had stingers.

They did and hurt like hell when released into someone's skin. There were so many things he would have done differently if he'd known. For one, he would have called his friend out so they could clear the air.

This wasn't the time to go into it. Besides, it was too late to do anything about it. Regret stabbed him and his thoughts immediately snapped to his father. Lawson wouldn't be able to live with himself if he didn't have the conversation with his father that needed to happen. The one where they cleared the air between them. He needed his old man to hang on and be well enough for the talk to happen.

Forcing his thoughts back to the present, he drove around the cul-de-sac. Backing up as though into a parking spot, he positioned the Jeep for an easy exit. He still had on his ankle holster with his backup weapon inside. The palm-sized Sig Sauer made for easy retrieval and use in an emergency. He'd been too hungry to fiddle with taking it off earlier when he'd changed out of his wet clothes.

"Does anything look different?" he asked. The lights were completely off inside the home, which struck him as odd.

"No, I cut the lights off because it was raining and I didn't want anyone to be able to track my movements while inside."

Smart. His brain added another adjective. *Beautiful.* The combination could be lethal because she was exactly his type.

Before they exited the vehicle, she reached over and touched his forearm. Long, lean fingers closed around his skin and a jolt of awareness shot through him faster than stray voltage.

"I probably shouldn't admit this to you, but that day in the honky tonk..."

She seemed to think better of finishing her sentence because suddenly her mouth clamped shut as she withdrew her hand. The warmth of her touch was replaced by a marked chill.

"Never mind," she finally said. "It's in the past where it belongs."

The curious side of him wanted to know exactly what she'd been about to say, whether she'd felt the connection between them that night the way that he had. The logical side warned him not to push it. Knowing wouldn't change anything, and the last thing he needed was another thing to add to his list of regrets.

"Let's go inside and figure out what's going on for Kevin's sake," he said, unsure why he'd just mentioned her deceased husband's name, except that he felt like he needed to put a little emotional distance between them. The move worked. He could almost see her wall that came up. As much as he tried to convince himself he was doing them a big favor, his heart protested. It made the argument that all he was doing was pushing another person away, keeping Eileen at arm's length.

Rather than go down that road mentally, he cut off the ignition before opening the Jeep's door. Kodo immediately followed, even when Lawson circled around the front of the vehicle to open Eileen's side. As usual, Kodo was right by Lawson's side. He didn't want to acknowledge the fact he'd come to rely on his canine partner for companionship or the obvious fact Kodo was the only one Lawson let get close to him, and Kodo wasn't even a person. Some might argue he was the closest thing to it without actually being human.

Before Lawson could get to the passenger door, it opened, and Eileen came out. She closed the door a little harder than was probably necessary, but Jeeps didn't need a hard swing. Or maybe she was working through his comment. Either way, this didn't seem like the right time to ask questions or point it out. The Jeep was fine, but the noise from the door slam might just wake the neighbors. This wasn't exactly the way to go in stealth. Neither was driving in the cul-de-sac with his Jeep, so he couldn't exactly talk.

Kodo stayed right by Lawson's side. He'd been so proud the moment Kodo didn't have to be leashed. Voice commands worked magic and the extra seconds it took to unhook a leash from his collar saved valuable time. It also kept Kodo safer. The sooner he caught a perp, the closer Lawson could be. Kodo had no fear and no idea when a gun was being pointed at him. He was trained to keep going. The vest he wore offered some protection against a bullet. Not enough as far as Lawson was concerned.

Eileen had been gripping the shoulder strap of her handbag. She dipped her hand inside as they approached the front door. The jangle of keys sounded loudly as the rain had stopped and there was no more thunder to serve as cover.

After unlocking the door, she stepped inside and into the darkness.

"Should I turn on the light?" she asked.

"Might as well," he said. After driving up in his Jeep, they weren't flying under the radar on this one. It might be for the best. The probability someone was inside the house at this exact moment was slim. Even if someone was here, Lawson didn't want them sticking around. This trip wasn't about busting anyone. It was about figuring out what Kevin had gotten himself involved in and why.

Light bathed the room as Kodo stood at attention besides Lawson. He gave the command for Kodo to investigate. The dog took off toward what Lawson assumed was the kitchen.

Looking around the room, he thought the place was cozy. The main wall in the living room was anchored by a fireplace. There was wood paneling on the walls, and it looked like a baby store had thrown up inside the house. The thought brought a small smile to his face.

"What?" Eileen asked. He didn't realize she'd been studying him.

"Nothing important," he said. "I'm just amazed at how much stuff one little baby requires. How old is this kid again?"

"Four months," she said, returning the smile. She waved a hand like she was presenting a new car. "And, yes, they come with a whole lot of accessories."

There was already a sofa and chair along with a coffee table in the room. Pretty much every inch seemed like it was filled with baby paraphernalia. There was a swing, a carrier, and a playpen, all in bright colors despite the warm tones of Eileen's furniture. The kid stuff stood out like a sore thumb in every bright color under the sun. There wasn't much on the walls. On the fireplace sat a picture of Kevin in his dress uniform, standing next to a flag. They all had that same picture, and yet it took on a new meaning when it was all someone had left of a loved one.

There were no photos of the two of them as a couple. He figured the picture of Kevin was more for his son to remember a fallen father than for Eileen to mourn a husband. Then again, it had been a year and she'd believed her husband was cheating on her. One picture on the mantel was probably being generous under the circumstances.

Aside from the kid stuff and the toys and blankets on the sofa, there were unpacked boxes. She'd clearly been too busy since moving in to finish decorating. Considering she'd been two months pregnant when Kevin had been killed, she'd done pretty well getting anything in the place at all. Again, guilt slammed into him for not being here to help. He *should* have.

"Where are the boxes?" he asked her. It was probably wrong of him to be relieved this wasn't the home she'd shared with Kevin. And yet, he was.

"They're in the master closet," she said. "There's a weird little space at the back of my closet where I tucked them for the time being. The pull-down ladder to the attic is broken, so I can't use the space until it's fixed."

"Old homes are fun," he said. He had plenty of experience raiding every kind of home, and the older ones ended up being the most interesting. Between the things he found inside walls to secret passages, he never took a floorplan for granted, unlike newer homes that seemed to all come from the same blueprint. High priced homes generally had some type of escape room or tornado shelter since Texas was known for those.

Even with the baby items scattered around, Eileen's place surprisingly felt like home. This seemed like a good time to remind himself that he didn't belong here with the home or with her.

Eileen noticed how attentive Lawson had been since she'd shown up at his home hours ago by this point. He seemed able to anticipate what she really needed before she even articulated it. Her relationship with Kevin had sparked a little bit in the early days and he'd been similarly considerate. Then it had fizzled into what she believed was settling into loving each other, rather than being in love. For reasons she couldn't explain, she knew in her heart that a spark with someone like Lawson would never burn out. He was the real deal of honesty, integrity, and honor. Those were traits she believed belonged to Kevin too.

Then, the little lies came.

He would make excuses for being late for work. He called in sick one day, told her that he couldn't get out of bed, and then when she circled back to check on him during her lunch break, he was gone. She didn't confront him about it. Instead, she asked how his day had been, checked his forehead, and then made soup for dinner. He'd told her that he couldn't get out of bed all day but was starting to feel better now that she was home. Then, there were the times he would tell her that he was running out to grab a six-pack and then not return for two hours. At times, he came home empty-handed. When she confronted him in the beginning, he would shower her with love and affection. It was almost like the early days of dating again. She recognized the distraction for what it was and filed the information away. Truth be told, she'd been looking into marriage counseling for them. He didn't like the idea one bit and shut her down quickly.

Everything about being with Lawson seemed genuine. The thought surprised her as she led him into her bedroom. She felt suddenly aware of the king-sized bed in the room and was thankful she'd pulled the covers up. The room was presentable. "Pardon the mess."

"You should see my place," he quickly countered in what had to be an effort to make her feel better.

She almost choked on a cough. "I did see your home. It was tidy."

"*Tidy?*" he asked, almost sounding offended at the compliment.

"Neat," she corrected. "You know, everything has a place. Except I wanted to put a coaster on your oak table, to protect it from getting a ring." Her cheeks heated at the admission. Why on earth did she feel the need to tell him that?

"For a minute there, I thought you were going to accuse me of being perfect or something and I can assure you that's not the case." This time, he cracked a small smile and her heart fluttered in her chest.

Hearts were wild things. There was a reason they were kept inside a rib*cage.* Hers betrayed her by squeezing every time Lawson was close enough to breathe in his unique scent. He smelled of spice and warmth. Eileen shook off the heady feeling that tried to take hold with Lawson standing next to her.

After locking gazes and then holding a few seconds too long, he refocused on the master closet. Old homes had big closets and this one was basically a whole wall. She opened the double doors. The closet slanted in the back, which seemed like a good place to tuck the boxes so she could access them when she wanted to but didn't have to look at them every day if she didn't. They were cardboard reminders of the life she was supposed to be living instead of being a widow and single mother in her early thirties.

She kneeled down and climbed in before pulling out boxes. There were four medium-sized moving boxes on this side. The few on the other side mostly had the clothing items she hadn't had the heart to donate, along with their wedding book. She'd tucked it inside the box when she decided not to throw it away, which she'd been tempted to do after the funeral while the cheating accusations swirled in her head. Was it worse to be a dirty cop or an unfaithful husband?

Lawson went to work on the boxes, opening the first. "Do you have any idea which one his laptop is in?"

"No," she said, shaking her head, realizing her answer didn't need to be so emphatic a couple of seconds too late. A simple 'no' would have done the trick. All her emotions were amped up, causing the word to come out charged. From the minute she'd been run off the road to showing up at Lawson's door to now, her pulse seemed to be on steroids.

Nails tapping on wood flooring in the hallway were followed by the sounds of panting. Kodo jogged into the room. It was probably a good sign he hadn't barked. There was no forgetting him either way or his presence.

"I'm thinking once this is all over, I should maybe get a dog," she said. Would it help fill the void that had been created when her husband had been killed?

"That's a good idea," Lawson responded. "I could help you find a good rescue."

"I'd like that a lot," she said, wondering how much she should share about her recent past. "This is probably going to come as a shock to you since Kevin became distant with everyone after we were married, including me, but our marriage wasn't on solid ground. I wish it had been, but it wasn't."

"I'm sorry to hear it," Lawson said. Based on the compassion in his tone, he meant those words too.

Could she let him be her temporary comfort?

CHAPTER SIX

Lawson moved beside Eileen as she sat back against the door. She'd brought her hand up to pinch her nose like she was trying to stave off a headache. His heart went out to her and her circumstances. "If it's any consolation, I know Kevin fell hard for you the second he saw you standing there in that cream-colored dress that fell right about here on your leg." He ran his finger across his leg about midthigh. You had on brown and teal boots that day and, despite the attire fitting in to a T, I don't think I've ever seen anyone look so out of her comfort zone in that bar.

Eileen broke into a smile.

"I was," she admitted. "And I only stuck around because..." She shook her head as though finishing the sentence wouldn't do either one of them any good. "None of that matters now. We are where we are. No regrets." She paused a couple of beats before raising her gaze to meet his. "And I wouldn't have Kevin Jr. if things had turned out differently. That little boy gave me a reason to wake up every morning, when I wanted to fold the tent, curl in a ball, and stop breathing."

It wasn't unnoticed by Lawson that she'd lost a sister when she was too young to truly understand the impact, and now she'd lost a husband before they'd had time to get their life together off the ground.

"Life can bite pretty hard and be the worst kind of unfair," he said, figuring that statement covered a whole lot of territory. "It seems to strike the hardest when we least expect or deserve it. And there isn't always a means to hit back except sheer stubbornness."

She nodded.

"And yet, you've found a way to keep going each time life tried to take you down," he continued. She needed to be reminded of her strength. "You keep fighting and getting up every day when it would have been easier to quit and have every right to do so."

"Thank you," she said, but her voice was small and almost fragile. She didn't quite believe in herself the way he did. He could hear it in her tone. "But I have little Kevin to think about. I can't curl up in a ball."

"You don't," he said. "There's a difference."

Her tongue slicked across her bottom lip, leaving a silky trail that he had no business staring at. Kodo nudged him. His canine partner always seemed to know when to shift Lawson's focus.

"Good, boy," he said to Kodo before giving the command to rest. Kodo moved to the door instead, almost as though he could sense trouble brewing. Lawson took note before turning his attention back to Eileen. "I don't know what we'll find in these boxes or how that might shape your opinion of Kevin, but I do know how hard he was hit when he first saw you."

"You were there too," she said softly, and there was a hint of rejection in her voice.

"Yes, but he saw you first," he stated.

"That's not true," she quickly countered before adding, "You made eye contact with me before Kevin."

"It doesn't matter now," he said to her.

"It does to me," she said in that quiet voice that acted as an armor-piercing missile straight to his heart. Yes, he'd seen her first and, although he didn't care to admit it now to anyone, least of all himself, his attraction to her had nearly knocked him off his boots.

"The bottom line is Kevin made the first move, and I had to respect it as his best friend," Lawson said, thinking how much he wished he could go back and change that moment. He'd thought about that moment far too many times over the past twenty-four months. So much so, he wished he could erase it from his thoughts completely.

"I wasn't a prize to be won or 'called' by anyone," she said with more than a hint of indignation.

"No, you weren't," he said. "But we were both...*interested*...and no one could have known how any of this was going to turn out. Do I have regrets?" He paused for a few beats. "Do birds sing?"

Eileen dropped her gaze to her hands that were twisting together. She shrugged. "I guess you're right. It doesn't make a difference now. We can't go back and I wouldn't change the past because now I have little Kevin to show for it."

"I'm sorry you didn't think you could tell me about

your son earlier," Lawson said, thinking the best way to preserve his friend's memory was through the little boy.

"He wanted you to be the godfather," she said quietly.

Those words were a bucket of ice after what felt like several shots of tequila. His throat burned, his stomach warmed, but the chill after shocked him back to reality.

"I would have said yes."

Lawson wasn't exactly sure why he felt the need to say those words out loud, except to say that he wanted her to know there were some things that came before his own desires. Those had him wishing he could step back in time and be the one to call off his buddy instead of the other way around. What had stopped him though? Kevin would have understood if Lawson had been the one to speak up first. There might have been disappointment. Of course. That was a certainty. Eileen was worth fighting for.

So why didn't he? Why did he walk away so easily? He almost laughed out loud at the last question. It hadn't been easy. He'd had a devil of a time trying to forget Eileen existed. There was something about her laugh that was like a spring breeze that followed a heavy rain, light enough to float through the air. There was something cleansing about breathing it in.

Since he was starting to wax poetic, he decided to give himself a mental headshake and move on to the first box. There were papers inside that had most likely come from a home office. Training certificates and commendations from early in Kevin's career. During a time like this, it was easy to forget Kevin had been a great officer.

Lawson sifted through the first couple of boxes, unable or unwilling to look too closely at the random photographs inside. His eye stopped on what looked like a honeymoon picture in a heart-shaped silver frame.

"I couldn't bring myself to throw those away." Eileen's voice cut through his melancholy. She was so much more than just physical beauty. He'd sensed it that night at the bar. To be honest, it had caught him off guard and scared the heck out of him. No one had ever hit him square in the chest with one look in the way she had. In one instant, he'd almost been knocked on his backside. That was a whole lot of power to willingly hand over to another human being. By the time he realized that might not be such a bad thing, Kevin had moved in on Eileen.

It had been his own fault. He had no one to blame but himself. And now he was paying the price and would forever, because an attraction like the one he felt with Eileen wasn't something that came around every day.

In the past two years, she had been the one he measured everyone else against. He could acknowledge that wasn't fair. And yet where was logic when it came to the heart? If someone could figure out how to infuse sense into emotion, he would sure like to shake the person's hand. It escaped him.

Meanwhile, he kept sifting through box contents until he located Kevin's laptop. "Found it."

"Maybe there will be a few answers there," Eileen said, with a trepidation in her voice that said she wasn't certain she wanted to know.

He held up the piece of technology and compressed his lips into a thin line. "Let's see."

There was a very large and growing part of Eileen that wanted to let sleeping dogs lie. Except the dog in question was not only awake but barking and about to bite anyone and anything in its path. Especially her. She sucked in a breath. "Let's do this."

Lawson opened the laptop and hit the power button. As she probably should have expected, there was no power. "I'm guessing the charger to this thing is somewhere in here," he said. Or, should I say that I'm hoping?"

"Hope is probably a good word," she conceded with a shrug. "I didn't throw anything away, but I couldn't tell you where it is."

He resumed the digging in boxes. "Not to change the subject, but as I search for the right cable, I'd like to know what it's like to be a parent. My mother died when I was too young to know better, and my father wasn't the paternal type. Has it changed you?"

"There are just so many ways that it's almost impossible to articulate them all," she stated with the kind of warmth and hope in her voice that made it seem like the future was so much brighter now. "Having a baby is such an amazing thing. It's hard to explain but suddenly your heart is beating outside your chest, and you realize just how small you are in comparison to the world around you. You also know instantly that you would do anything to nurture and protect this little thing that is dependent on you for every aspect of life. Literally, the little bean couldn't survive a day without you. And it makes you seem surprisingly small in the whole context of life."

"Sounds like it transforms just about every part of you," he said after a few beats while he considered those words. Was it the same for a father?

"True," she admitted. "But then, it also made me wonder why my parents didn't seem to have the same reaction to parenting. You know?"

"I guess not everyone gets the gene," he said before adding, "whatever that means. All I can say is that my father didn't get it."

"Neither of my parents seemed to either," she immediately said. "Having little Kevin made me understand how difficult the job is in some ways and in others, it just made me mad. I wondered how my parents could have held something so little in their arms and then not protected it. I get that they loved my sister and the loss was unimaginable. But they still had another daughter and I seemed to disappear into the world of their work after the accident that claimed Andrea's life."

"One who needed them very much," he added as though he knew firsthand.

"Yes," she agreed. "And, I guess, it's just really difficult to forgive them for neglecting me when I was still alive, barely six years old, and needed them more than anything."

"It's strange, isn't it?" he asked, but the question was clearly meant to be rhetorical. "After my father lost my mother, he seemed to lose all sense of family too. I mean, I can only assume that's what happened since I was too young to remember. But I kept wondering why he bothered to have a family at all if he had no intention of stepping up. We needed him to do just that, and he went into his own shell, burying himself in work."

"I get these things are hard and, believe me when I say life can gut you," she continued, realizing they'd both suffered losses at a young age. Was it part of the reason they'd connected so instantly and intensely? Two broken souls that had found each other? "But little Kevin is exactly what motivates me. I keep thinking of how he will see me in five or ten years. I keep thinking about what kind of person I want him to see is and then I go for it. Why couldn't my parents to do the same? Or your father?"

"Because you're special," he said, and his voice dropped a couple of octaves when he spoke. There was a rusty quality to his deep timbre now, for lack of a better description. It was gravelly and, she had to admit, sexy. But then Lawson Quinn had always been sex on a stick. The man was gorgeous beyond what good looks should be. He had all the qualities she wanted little Kevin to inherit; honesty, kindness, brains. The fact Lawson was wrapped in one helluva package didn't hurt his appeal. But she couldn't think of herself as special and survive the day-to-day.

"I'm not," she argued. "And I'd rather you not say it."

"Why?" he asked before seeming to catch himself. "Never mind. Don't answer that. It's easy to see that you think everyone is built like you, but they're not. You're special, whether you like it or not."

"I'd rather not think of myself that way," she said. "Special doesn't get you anywhere. Hard work is a different story. Special and a nickel is worth five cents. The ability to work hard and not rely on luck is a better deal any day of the week."

She saw a whole conversation play out in his eyes, but he clamped his mouth shut rather than speak further. She suspected he was about to argue his side and offer more proof that she was unique, but she wasn't having it. She meant what she said. She would take hard work over being special. Special made folks lazy.

Instead of arguing, Lawson dug around in another box before locating the right power cord to Kevin's laptop. She had tried a couple of times to get past the password screen on Kevin's laptop but decided not to get locked out if she failed a third time. His personal phone had the same deal. The pregnancy had made her sick, losing her husband had made her sad, and she kept putting off digging into Kevin's devices. There was probably a piece of her that didn't really want to know if her husband had been having an affair while she was pregnant. Not knowing made it easier to believe the love they'd shared had been real and had meant something. There'd been no other reason to marry, otherwise except that they'd been two loners.

Were they both searching for a family that didn't exist? Trying to create one out of an attraction?

Kevin had family in Louisiana that he wasn't close to. She got the impression his stepfather had been a jerk toward him. There was no love lost between him and the man his mother had married. He spoke fondly of his sister, admitting they had mostly a social media relationship. The rare times he was on social media, he would search out her posts and make sure to like them. The ten-year age gap between them didn't help bring them any closer. It didn't help that his parents handed her everything on a silver platter while telling him that he needed to work for what he got. The double standard didn't sit well. His sister pulled the 'pampered pet' card a little too often when she was young and bratty. The two had grown closer a few years ago, according to Kevin. Even so, they weren't exactly best friends like Eileen remembered being with her sister.

Wow, she hadn't thought about their friendship in a very long time. Had she suppressed the memories so they wouldn't tear her heart into pieces? Her parents had been shredded. Rightfully so in some ways. Now that Eileen had become a mother, she could be more forgiving in some ways. In others, she was torn. Her instincts to protect little Kevin were stronger than anything she'd ever felt. Holding her seven-pound newborn in her arms had changed her quicker than a finger snap. The second she laid eyes on her son, it was over for her. She would never look at the world in the same way again. Part of her felt bad for this little guy, because she'd had no support system and no idea what she was doing until Millie knocked on the door with a plate of food and a lifetime's worth of earned advice.

Despite the fact Millie didn't have children of her own, she'd become an aunt several times over and took the role seriously, as she'd put it. Eileen wouldn't have made it through those last few months of pregnancy or early colicky weeks without Millie's support and guidance. The kind neighbor had been a godsend, going so far as to stop over at four o'clock in the morning after waking up, so Eileen could sleep. Millie even brewed her own coffee so as not to make any noise.

As much as Eileen might want to change many events of the past year, give or take, she wouldn't change having little Kevin or getting to know Millie. Life was made up of good and bad. No one got a free pass. And she'd experienced immense joy over the last few months, as well as intense pain.

"I'm in," Lawson said, interrupting her revelry. "Let's see if there's anything in here to give us a trail to work with, so we can make progress on who might be watching you and trying to run you off the road."

"Hold on a second, Lawson." She held her hand up to stop him. He froze and locked gazes with her. "I can't do this right now."

CHAPTER SEVEN

"What is it?" Lawson's fingers stopped mid-type. He figured her, of all people, would be eager to find out what was on the personal laptop of her dead husband that might have brought trouble to her door. One look at her gave him the explanation he was searching for. She twisted her fingers together in a braid, and her facial expression was rife with fear. She was scared of what she would find.

"I don't know," she hedged, but her concern was written all over the deep grooves in her forehead.

When he opened Kevin's e-mail or personal files, they might get confirmation that he was dirty or at the very least involved in sketchy dealings. Right now, Kevin was still a hero until proven otherwise. Lawson had similar thoughts after breaking the password protection. He was handy with computers, which had helped. But he also knew Kevin. The password had been his and Eileen's wedding date. Should he tell her that? Would knowing most folks used an important date as a password ease her concerns about how much he'd loved her?

Probably not when he really thought about it. The date might be important, and Lawson had no doubts that Kevin had been in love with Eileen, but that didn't mean he wasn't cheating. Kevin's instant attraction might not have been real love. The kind that took time to build. Relationships weren't created in one day or based on a passing attraction.

Once again, the annoying voice in the back of his mind said that someone like Eileen was not a casual affair for anyone. She wasn't the type to jump in with both feet, which was one of many reasons Lawson had been shocked by their quick engagement and even faster wedding. Pregnancy would have made for an easy explanation. Except that she hadn't been pregnant at the time of either event. Lawson wondered why they'd rushed into becoming a family when they'd been married less than a year.

Eileen stood up. Her stress levels seemed to be climbing. Kodo took note. His ears shot up and forward. His muscles tensed like he was getting ready for action. Lawson gave his partner the command to stand down. Kodo did, but he was like a tightly coiled snake ready to spring into action on a moment's notice.

Lawson pushed to standing, setting the laptop down next to his partner. He stepped aside as Eileen paced. She stopped right in front of him and looked at him with danger in her eyes. There was a whole lot of need —need that was reciprocated. Common sense told him to step away before something happened she might regret. Where was practical thinking in a time like this?

Right now, all rationale flew out the window when he breathed in her unique scent. It was a mix of fragrant spring wildflowers and lemon.

She stood there, looking up at him as the air crackled with electricity in the space between them. There was no way he would be able to pull off a nonchalant reaction with her standing this close. No way to stop his pulse from racing. No way to keep his pupils from dilating or force his breathing to slow down. Not with Eileen.

"I'd like to kiss you, but I'm afraid you'll think it's a bad idea," she said, and her voice was soft and vulnerable. How was he supposed to turn her down?

"It would be," he agreed, "however, those words could never come out of my mouth."

If she wanted permission to kiss him, he couldn't give it. That had to be up to her. Lawson was up to his eyeballs with regret. His relationship with his father, for one. Also topping the list was not telling his buddy that Lawson had seen her first. It would have been so easy for him to stop Kevin at the bar. A few words would have done the trick and he could have saved everyone from a whole lot of heartache. He didn't want to believe that Kevin would cheat on his wife, despite the fact his buddy was a known flirt at work and at all their usual haunts. Flirting was one thing. Acting on it was a different ballgame altogether.

What was the difference? a little voice in the back of his mind asked. In truth, he couldn't come up with a defense for it. A married man shouldn't be flirting with anyone else. It was disrespectful to his wife and vice versa. Lawson had dated a couple of flirts in his day.

There was nothing worse than returning to a table to see his date flirting with single guys at the bar. He didn't have an instinct to puff out his chest as if to say *she's with me.* To him, it meant a fast ride home and a quick trip to the never-date-again list.

"What did you decide?" she asked, cutting into his mental debate.

"I'm not in the right state of mind to make a decision about you...us," he said. "And yet kissing you would be right up there with one of the best things that ever happened to me." It might be the past talking or all that stored up regret. Either way, he didn't have the energy to fight his feelings for her any longer. This was exactly the reason he hadn't called her in the past year. He didn't trust himself. Knowing Kevin hadn't treated her in the way he should have wasn't helping Lawson win the fight against the overwhelming urge to bring her into his arms and be her comfort.

"You're a respectable person, Lawson. I trust you to make the right call." Her tongue slicked across her bottom lip, drawing attention to a small freckle just to the left of her full lips.

"No one's perfect, Eileen. Especially not me," he countered as she brought her hands up and then placed them on his chest. The thin cotton of his t-shirt did nothing to absorb the jolt of electricity that came with contact. Her fingers twitched before she pressed them deeper against him. He brought his hands up to cover hers with the idea that he would remove them. In reality, his hands felt too good against her skin to be able to think clearly. A fog overtook his brain, clouding his judgment in the best possible way.

The part of him that wanted to kiss her more than breathe said there was no harm in taking what she was so willing to give. Before he could talk himself out of it, he dropped his lips down on hers. Tiny tingles reverberated through his exposed skin where it touched hers.

Heat threatened to consume him as she parted her lips and teased his tongue inside her mouth. His pulse shot through the roof as he brought his hands up to cup her face, positioning her lips for better access.

A bomb detonated inside his chest as his heart battered the inside of his ribcage. He'd never experienced a kiss like this one before despite having a whole lot of experience. He seemed to know on instinct that kissing Eileen would raise the bar. There'd be no going back after this, which he tried to convince himself that he'd be fine with. Finding her and losing her before anything could get started, then watching her with his best friend had nearly ripped his heart from his chest.

The annoying voice in the back of his mind picked this moment to point out that he'd seen her first. He'd fallen for her first. And he'd waited a long time for this to happen. Had he though? Had he waited? Because that same voice whispered into his ear, telling him that he was still in love with her.

Kodo jumped to attention and started rapid-fire barking. Lawson pulled back, rotating so he could tuck Eileen behind him as he faced the doorframe. His partner was ready to jump out of his skin. Containing him when he was this worked up could prove a challenge.

Guilt stabbed Lawson for allowing himself to be distracted when he should be on full alert, keeping

Eileen safe. He bent down and quickly retrieved his backup weapon from the ankle holster. Holding the weapon out in front of him at his eye line, he started toward the hallway leading to the front door where Kodo was pointed with his whole being.

"I'll be right back," Lawson turned and whispered to Eileen.

"You're not going without me," she stated in a tone that left no room for argument. If this was official business, he would have to follow protocol and leave her behind. Since this was personal and *her* home, he wouldn't disagree.

Lawson took a couple of steps before he was out of the bedroom. Kodo was barely contained as the coil seemed to tighten a little more with each step. He was trained to go on Lawson's command, but these types of dogs had an air of unpredictability about them. Unleashing the coil made them good at their jobs.

"Eileen?" an uncertain-sounding older female voice floated down the hallway.

"It's Millie," Eileen said with a sigh. "It's okay."

Lawson bit back a curse. Was he about to come face-to-face with his former best friend's kid?

"Back here," Eileen shouted to Millie as she tried to force a calm she didn't feel. First of all, there'd been the kiss that had basically reset her clock and changed her expectations of what a kiss should make her feel for the rest of her life. Then, there was the surprise visit. Did she really want Millie meeting her in the bedroom while

Lawson was here? He'd stopped at the door and lowered his gun. "Hold on a minute. I'm coming."

She gave a Lawson a look that he seemed to understand. He nodded and turned back toward the laptop, calling Kodo to stay by his side.

"I'll make sure everything is okay and be right back," she said to him. At this point, she didn't want to have to explain everything to Millie. The break-in was only 'suspected' at this point and she couldn't find anything missing, not that she'd inventoried all of Kevin's belongings. She hadn't. Like Lawson had pointed out, there was no real proof even though trusting her gut was the right thing to do. She needed to exercise caution and assume her home had been violated. The thought caused bile to rise, burning the back of her throat.

Making her way to the living room, before Millie could get to the bedroom first, Eileen tried her best to calm her racing heart. The second she stepped into the room, Millie held up her phone. Eileen had expected to see little Kevin and was relieved he wasn't going to be around her while she was worked up like this. Babies seemed to pick up on their mothers' moods and she didn't want him to feel her fear.

"Everything okay?" she asked Millie.

"He's sleeping like the angel he is," the older woman quickly reassured. Millie's long hair was always piled up in a loose bun on top of her head, making her seem taller than five-feet-two-inches. She had that wholesome grandmotherly look that would make a great advertisement for all-natural oatmeal or pancake syrup.

"Did he have a good evening?" she asked, missing holding her little boy in her arms.

"Yes, but when did you get a dog?" Millie cut right to the chase.

"A friend is visiting," she stated.

"That explains the Jeep," Millie noted.

"He was Kevin's best friend," Eileen felt the need to explain. "He's helping me go through Kevin's personal effects to see what I should keep and what I can discard."

"That explains the look on your face," Millie stated. There was no way Eileen planned to dig deeper into those words. Besides, it was true. The look on her face had everything to do with going through Kevin's things, being here with Lawson, and him helping her. There was no reason to overexplain to Millie, even though she was the one who'd recently told Eileen that she needed to think about moving on and picking her life up. Millie had said Eileen was too young to fold up the tent and never date again. Would she approve of Eileen and Lawson? They weren't exactly dating so the point was mute, and yet she couldn't stop herself from wondering...

"Like you said, it might be time to think about the next chapter," she explained. She held back the part about not truly being able to close off the last one until she knew who was following her and why. She didn't want to scare the older woman. Knowing whether or not Kevin had been cheating might help close that door forever. Truth be told, the minute she'd suspected him of seeing other women during their marriage, she'd closed off part of her heart to him. A wall had come up that would never be knocked down completely. Most of the time, when her gut told her something, it ended up being true. Hers had screamed affair.

"That's good," Millie said. "Does 'moving on' mean a dog will be involved?"

Perceptive. It was hard to get one over on someone as savvy as Millie. She'd lived long enough to see right through the bull in the world.

"Lawson worked with Kevin," was all she said. She'd already mentioned the best friend part and Millie hadn't seemed phased in the least. She needed to change the subject or Millie would keep digging until there were no more secrets left. "How did little Kevin eat tonight?"

"Good," Millie said after a long pause. She smiled. "He burped just fine after his bottle and then fell asleep right on schedule."

He was finally big enough to sleep through the night, which was a godsend.

"Two weeks of seven hours at night is a welcome changed from the colicky baby I brought home," Eileen said with affection. She planned to tell Millie every day how much she appreciated everything she'd done, and was still doing, for her and little Kevin. "The change is thanks to you. We wouldn't have survived if you hadn't been there."

"It's no trouble at all." Millie swatted her hand like she was casually swatting a fly. "I'll head back over then. You said you wouldn't be home tonight and then I saw a light on, so I decided to make sure everything was all right."

"All good here," Eileen reassured. While she had her neighbor's attention, she figured she might as well ask about tomorrow too. "Any chance Kevin can stay with you all day tomorrow? I might be moving some of these boxes, so I'd rather roll up my sleeves on my day off and knock this out."

"Take all the time you need. In fact, why don't you take the next couple of days to finish dealing with this? I know it's been hanging over your head for a while now. With little Kevin around, you can't get anything done except care for him, considering how often he feeds while he's awake," Millie said.

"I do have work to think about," Eileen responded, hoping this didn't drag out over days.

"You were just talking about Claire hitting you up for more hours," Millie continued. "Maybe this is a good time to take her up on it."

"I'll think about it," Eileen conceded. "You're a lifesaver."

"You might not say that when you get my bill," Millie teased with a wide smile. "Be careful around that animal back there."

Eileen didn't hide her shock at the warning. "Oh?"

"He sounded fierce," Millie said.

Oh, right, she was talking about Kodo. For a second there, Eileen thought Millie was referring to Lawson. He was dangerous in a different way. To her heart. She'd been disappointed by him before. Let the attraction simmering between them go much further and she could end up shattered. She'd already lost hope in the relationship that was supposed to be for life, after suspecting an affair. When she'd married Kevin, it had been for the long haul. Even though he was gone for a different reason now, she couldn't ignore the writing had been on the wall for her marriage. She'd wanted counseling. Kevin had said they were fine and it might make him look bad with the department.

Trust wasn't high on her list right now.

"Good protection, though," Eileen stated, forcing her focus back to Millie.

"Keep me posted on what you end up doing," Millie said before heading toward the front door.

Eileen followed and then locked it behind her neighbor. By the time she made it back to the master bedroom, her pulse had settled down a few notches. Until she saw the look on Lawson's face.

Her heart dropped. "What did you find?"

CHAPTER EIGHT

"I'm sorry." Those were the weakest words when it came to expressing how Lawson felt, but they were the only two he could come up with in the moment.

"Cheating?" Eileen asked. It was more statement than question, so he didn't...*couldn't*...bring himself to answer. "How many were there?"

Lawson stopped himself right there. If the shoe were on the other foot, he wasn't sure he would want to know. What could be done about it? Eileen wouldn't be able to confront Kevin. The knowledge certainly couldn't make her feel better about the life she had been sharing with her husband. What good could come out of this knowledge?

Except that on a base level he realized that he would want to know. He would want to know if the love had been real.

"Are you absolutely sure you want to know this?" he asked.

"Without question," she responded with no hesitation.

"Okay. Based on the e-mail account he'd been hiding. One," he said. "But it was serious." Would a casual affair hurt less? Somehow, he doubted it. Infidelity was still infidelity whether there was half a dozen or one, whether it was serious or a one-and-done.

"What's her name?" she continued. Again, the information would only hurt at this point but he realized he would have asked the same question.

"Liz Fox," he stated. "Could be a made-up name though."

"Can you dig up personal information about her?" she continued.

"I can tell you that she works at a bar and that he didn't feel good about what he was doing," he informed, knowing full well it wouldn't dull the pain.

"He said that?"

"In so many words," he said.

"What did he say exactly?" Anger and disappointment rolled off Eileen in palpable waves, not that he blamed her one bit.

"He told her that you got pregnant and that they should break it off. Said none of this was supposed to happen and that he didn't want to hurt you," he continued on a heavy sigh.

"So the affair started before I got pregnant?" she asked, but she already knew it did. She probably just needed a minute to process.

He nodded.

"Said he didn't have anyone else to talk to and that she was a good listener," he said, hating that he had to be the one to break the news to her and provide details that were so clearly breaking her heart.

"Why wouldn't they text? Why do this over e-mail?" The question seemed like it was meant to be rhetorical but there was an answer here for that as well.

"Kevin told her in an earlier e-mail that he couldn't give out his personal cell number and that he would buy a burner phone. He said it would be too easy to get lazy and reach out via text or a call, and that he wanted to protect you from what was happening as much as possible," he continued, despising being the one to deliver this news.

"Do you think the number I called belonged to her?" she asked.

"That's a good question," he said. "Her husband might have been monitoring her calls. She might have had other affairs."

"How do you know she was married?" she asked.

He pointed to the laptop.

"Of course," she said. "The two of them seemed to talk about everything. Why wouldn't they both be married? Plus, wasn't that so much easier? Less risk of entanglement?"

"They met online from what I could gather. He was seeking advice and the two of them connected. She happened to work nearby. She worked at night and told him to stop by after work so they could talk in person," he said, not answering her rhetorical questions. Only Kevin knew his reasons for why he'd chosen this person to have an affair with and Lawson didn't want to guess what they were.

"Seems like a coincidence," she said.

"We don't know what site they met on."

"True," she agreed. "Maybe he was on a hookup site. You can get everything on the internet nowadays. Maybe that's how they met."

She crossed her arms over her chest and rubbed her arms like the temperature had dropped forty degrees and she was staving off the sudden chill. He could only imagine what she was thinking and feeling after having one of her worst fears confirmed. He could see it in her eyes and on her features. Being the one to deliver the news wasn't high on his list of happiest moments. In fact, this was the pits.

"I'm not sure," he finally said, slowing down the conversation so she could have a minute to digest the news. "I'm just sorry any of this happened to you."

"Thank you," she said. "I'd asked him to go to counseling to figure out what changed between us."

"Guilt, for one thing," he said as he continued to skim more of the e-mail exchanges. "Hold on. There's more here."

She took in an audible breath as if to say *what now?*

"Looks like she was blackmailing him," he continued as he read to the bottom of one of their last exchanges. "She threatened to confront you and tell you all about their affair if he didn't help her out of some kind of situation."

Eileen sat down on the bed. The mattress dipped under her weight. "Did she say what she wanted from him?"

He shook his head.

"The e-mails stopped shortly after he told her they had to meet in person. He didn't want to keep talking about it online. He requested a face-to-face," he said before checking the date of the last e-mail. "This came two days before he was shot."

"The person who was accused of killing him swore he didn't do it. Said there was no gun found on him, even though witnesses said otherwise," she whispered. "No one believed him because a witness picked him out of a lineup. Said he was there and pointing the weapon."

"Most criminals lie about having a gun. The call Kevin was responding to was a fight at Zilker Park," he recounted the details from the day. "Witnesses reported hearing multiple gunshots, but no one could find anything other than knives on the people involved. This group wasn't known for shootings, but it had happened on occasion. Plus, fights have a way of escalating. There'd been rumors of a power struggle within the ranks. The shooter would have ditched the weapon. When they found out a cop had been killed, they would have denied their own mother to save their hides from going to jail on a capital murder charge."

"How did you get all this so quickly?" she asked. "We were just talking about trying to get access to the report a few hours ago."

"I texted a buddy who remembered some details. The last thing I wanted to do was open the file officially," he explained. "Not unless we have evidence and have run out of other possible explanations."

She nodded.

"Speaking of details, it makes sense that criminals don't make the most reliable witnesses," she agreed.

"Not when it means being locked up for the rest of their lives or going to the electric chair," he pointed out.

"The person who shot him must have known where he was or that he would be the one to respond to the call," she said. "Seems like a stretch, doesn't it?"

"Unless the person was already with him or supposed to meet up. Some folks monitor police communications. The individual might have used the fight as an opportunity to make the shot and then slip away unseen in the crowd that had gathered. Most witnesses would be watching the action and not the people fleeing. Folks would be running scared at the sound of shots being fired," he pointed out. "It seemed clear-cut that Kevin was shot while answering the call, so no one would think too much about crossfire despite being told otherwise."

"The internal investigators didn't find anything suspect," she said.

"Kevin was being extorted. Someone was threatening him. And then he ended up killed supposedly in crossfire," he said. "The whole scenario sounds suspect to me now that we know about the affair and the extortion. Internal investigations didn't have this information to go on."

"His back might have been against the wall or maybe he refused to go along with the blackmail, so they took him out," she reasoned.

"It's possible," he said with no conviction in his voice. "Did he act strange to you in the last few months before..." he let his voice trail off. She knew what he was getting at without him spelling it out again.

"Like what? Drugs?"

He nodded.

"No, he didn't," she said. "But then he was spending

more and more time in the garage. He was always tinkering with something he was trying to put together for the baby's room. You've seen all the gadgets needed to take care of little ones."

"There would be no reason to kill him if he refused to help someone or aid a criminal because they would lose their leverage," he reasoned. "They might have come after you in that case to force his hand."

"Now that you put it like that, it doesn't make sense to kill him at all," she said.

"He might have had a bout of conscience and told her that he was going to come clean with you and slash or the department or both," he continued along with that reasoning. "We know what he was asked to do must have been illegal. It's possible he didn't do anything at all and then threatened to arrest her or have her arrested."

"This woman might have been working with a partner," Eileen said. "Someone who has a military cut."

"It's a shame we don't know what she asked of Kevin." He double-checked the e-mails to see if there was a clue. There wasn't.

"Do you think she used her real name?" she asked.

"Maybe not. Liz Fox could have been made up. She told him to meet her at work, though. We can go digging around there as soon as I find the name of the place," he said, checking Kevin's browsing history. Bingo. "I have the name of a small bar on 5th Street. It's a popular place called Mustache Bar."

"Will Kodo be all right going with us?" she asked.

"We'll have to figure it out," he admitted. "I can't go asking around officially, so you'll have to be the one to do it. I'll coach you through what questions to ask. You're a beautiful woman, so all you have to do is cozy up to a male bartender." He put up a hand. "I know it sounds sexist but, believe me, it will work in an environment like this one."

"It is sexist," she agreed. "What if she sees me first? She must know what I look like. Right?"

"Not necessarily," he said. "I doubt Kevin would show his mistress pictures of his wife."

"I'm on his cell phone, though," she said. "Our wedding picture used to be his screensaver."

"What did you do with it, by the way?" he asked. "I didn't see his cell in the boxes so far."

"It's in the nightstand," she admitted. "I didn't think twice about boxing up his laptop. I was doing that anyway since I was moving. His cell phone felt a lot more personal, so I held onto it in my purse for a while. I would call and listen to his recorded voice while holding it in my hand. It made me feel a connection in a strange way. Like his hand had been here, holding this same thing, a few days, weeks, or months ago." She dropped her gaze. "We had problems and he might have turned to someone else, but I loved him. It might not be the way..."

She seemed to think better of finishing her sentence as she shook her head. "Point being, I never would have married him if I didn't have strong feelings for him that I thought had a chance at going the distance."

Hearing those words might sting, but he respected her even more for saying them.

"That might make me a fool," she continued.

"Loving someone even though it doesn't work out doesn't make you a fool," he quickly corrected.

Eileen didn't bring up the fact falling in love with the wrong person does. She understood and appreciated his perspective. He was bringing reason into matters of the heart, essentially saying no one was a fool for opening their heart to someone. In her case, she wasn't so sure. The wild part was that she'd been interested in Lawson, not Kevin. The spark she'd felt with Lawson was on another stratosphere. But then he'd stepped aside, and Kevin won her over. She convinced herself that sparks also led to out-of-control wildfires, and wildfires didn't last. They burned everything in their paths and then moved on. All she had to do to find another real-life example was look to her parents' love for each other and for her sister, and how much intense love like that damaged them when she died. She'd reasoned the same would happen to her attraction to Lawson, and it scared her to even think about leaning into that kind of love herself.

And as it turned out, Kevin wasn't the stable choice after all.

She checked the clock. "We'd better get going if we're going to make it to the Mustache Bar before closing." She wasn't doing herself any good contemplating the past or what might have been. She'd married Kevin and now had a beautiful baby boy out of the deal. She would never regret the path that brought her to motherhood and work at the nursery that she loved.

"All right," was all he said despite the questions playing out across his features.

She retrieved Kevin's cell phone, touched the framed photo of her infant son that was sitting on the same dresser, and then followed Lawson outside at a safe distance to give Kodo plenty of room. He stopped long enough to take care of business before Lawson grabbed a bottle of water and cupped his hands for a makeshift bowl. He bent down and gave his partner the contents. He started around to her side of the vehicle but she opened the door and climbed inside before he made it halfway.

It was close to midnight at this point, so the bar scene should be in full swing by the time they arrived. The drive over was spent in companionable silence. Lawson found a parking spot on the street two blocks over, which was a miracle in and of itself.

"Your best bet is to find a male bartender like I mentioned before and ask about employment opportunities. Casually mention that your friend Liz Fox said it's a great place to work and you decided to stop by to see if they have any openings. Try not to be obvious while you gauge his reaction to what you're saying." His advice was solid.

"I'm not sure I can pull this off, Lawson. I don't work in law enforcement and I'm a terrible liar."

"Any time you get nervous, just picture little Kevin's face," he said. "Remember why you're there and remember to breathe. Focus on those two things and you'll do fine."

She nodded. It sounded good while she was sitting

here. Could she go through with it and be convincing without Lawson standing beside her?

"If this doesn't sound like something you can do, we'll figure out another plan," he offered.

"How? We don't have time," she reasoned.

"We'll make it," he countered. "We can figure out another angle."

"It'll take more time, though, right?"

"Yes," he answered.

"In the meantime, I'm in danger and so is little Kevin," she continued.

"Potentially," he stated. "The person watching you hasn't made a real move."

"Yet."

She realized she'd scored a direct hit with that word the second Lawson's lips compressed into a frown. As much as she appreciated him for wanting to make this as easy as possible for her, she had to face it and figure out a way to push through her fears. Besides, running her off the road wasn't exactly doing nothing.

"I can do this," she reassured. "I *will* do this."

"Okay then," he said. "Give me your phone first."

She dug around in her handbag before producing her cell and getting him past the password protection screen. "Here you go."

He entered his cell number into her contacts. "Just in case you need me."

"Will you be right here the whole time?"

"I'll take Kodo out on leash to scope out the area. It'll give me an excuse to be nearby in case this thing goes south," he said. Those last words weren't exactly reassuring but they were honest. He was preparing her for the possibility something could go wrong. "We have no idea what you're walking into, Eileen. Keep your guard up."

"I will," she said before taking her cell phone back and then reaching for the door handle.

"And, Eileen," he stated.

"Yeah," she responded as she exited the Jeep. She turned to face him.

"For the record, I never would have been unfaithful." His words came out so low that she almost couldn't hear them.

"I know," was all she said before turning her attention to the task at hand. Physically, her stomach churned at the thought of facing the woman who'd been sleeping with Eileen's husband behind her back. There were so many questions and insecurities flooding her. Wasn't she enough for Kevin? Logically, she realized that wasn't why he'd cheated but emotions defied reason. And then there was the notion her workup about this visit would be for nothing. Liz Fox had been a made-up name, most likely. This bar was in Kevin's search engine but that didn't mean it was *the* bar where he met his mistress.

After using much of her remaining resolve to keep her feet moving toward the bar, she could only hope the visit wouldn't turn out to be a bust. Then again, she wouldn't have to wait long to find out.

CHAPTER NINE

Lawson leashed Kodo before exiting the vehicle. His partner normally drew a lot of attention, especially when they weren't in uniform. Kodo's ears were forward, on alert. His eyes were ever watchful. He'd become comfortable around Eileen in a short time. But then, Kodo took cues from Lawson. Both watched as she rounded the corner and then disappeared.

Heading the opposite direction, Lawson scanned the faces of the people on the streets. Austin was home to the University of Texas, which dumped fifty thousand young people on the streets, most of whom seemed to be out walking all the time. When a semester was in session, sidewalks were crowded and the pride of burnt orange practically glowed all the way to space.

"Can I pet your dog?" a young woman asked who was decked out in school colors.

"He's not friendly," Lawson said, causing disappointment to replace her smile. "Sorry."

"Does he bite?" she asked.

“Sometimes,” he answered honestly.

“Ah, okay,” she said, seeming satisfied with his response. “Too bad. He’s beautiful.”

“He’s a rescue,” he said, figuring the excuse wasn’t a complete lie. In many ways, the pair had rescued each other.

“Come on, Breanna,” one of the other young women called as the gaggle of what looked like teenagers crossed the street with their friend. “The line to Taco Shop is already around the block and they’re closing in an hour.”

Breanna smiled before taking off to be with her friends. Lawson had seen this scenario play out for all the years he’d lived and worked in Austin. Going to college was most young folks first time away from home. The novelty of being able to walk around all night if they wanted to, with no one to call them home and no curfew, had them running around at all hours. He’d dated a grad student once when he was younger who’d explained that quite a few freshmen washed out because they couldn’t stay out all night and keep up with their grades. Personally, he would have worked all night at a bar or washed dishes before he’d tucked his tail between his legs and gone home. He’d gotten a part-time job, worked his way through a much less expensive bachelor’s degree by knocking out his basics at community college, and attended a satellite school to finish out.

Then again, college had been on his dime because he’d refused to use any inheritance. It probably made a huge difference in level of commitment. There was no chance he was going to flunk out, especially since the cost seemed to skyrocket even more since he’d graduated. He couldn't even imagine trying to do the same thing today without taking out loans. He'd managed to get his education without going into debt, which he also realized was not the norm. It was probably his ranch upbringing that made it next to impossible for him to put himself in a position to owe anyone. Self-reliance had been ingrained in him.

Making a couple of lefts, he turned onto 5th Street. The distraction with the college kid kept him from rounding the corner at the same time, albeit opposite ends of the street, as Eileen. It had worked well, considering she was turning to step into the bar.

Her being out of sight wasn't a warm and fuzzy feeling for him, so he turned his attention to scanning folks on the street instead. Strangely, or maybe not so unexpectedly, someone with a military cut came around from the back of the bar and jogged across the busy street after looking both ways. He leaned against a building and lit a smoke. Was this the guy who'd been following Eileen?

Lawson took out his cell phone and, being as low-key as possible, took a couple of pics. It was nighttime and the pictures would turn out grainy at this distance plus he couldn't use his flash feature without giving himself away. The guy was standing near enough to the light it was possible to get something workable out of the shots. He would take what he could get at this point and see if he could turn it into a lead.

Someone like Military Cut would realize Lawson worked in law enforcement in a heartbeat. Could he get closer without being caught?

Eileen tossed her hair back, dabbed a little color on her lips, and then dropped the lipstick container into her handbag after stepping inside the crowded bar. Between throngs of people, she took note of a jukebox in the corner and a postage-stamp-sized dance floor. The bar was long and curved around in an L-shape. The name of the establishment made sense as she looked around. There were party bowls filled with fake mustaches strategically placed throughout. Several were on the bar, she noted, as she made her way through the crowd.

The woman who'd had an affair with Kevin might be in the room right now. The thought sat hard on her chest. She squared her shoulders to diffuse some of the weight.

Three bartenders seemed to be working double-time making all types of drinks. There was a woman and two men working the bar with what looked like two barbacks. Eileen had been on a couple dates with a bartender after sneaking in with a fake ID in her early college years. The job was more exhausting than it looked. A few of the drinks here looked more like science lab experiments. Others were regular cocktails plus a whole array of beers. Most of the customers seemed to be playing along with the mustache party favors, holding them up above their mouths. She grabbed the first one she could get her fingers on and did the same as she squeezed in between two men who had their backs to each other.

Conversation was like a contest of who could shout over the background noise the loudest. There was laughter, which was something she could acknowledge she'd had far too little of in recent years. In life?

Eileen conceded. She rarely laughed anymore. Not much had seemed funny.

Seeing all the people here, crammed into the space, laughing and having a good time hit her square in the chest.

"What can I get you?" a male voice boomed over the chatter.

"A job application?" She lowered the moustache.

His gray eyes lit up.

"When can you start?" he asked with a laugh.

"When do you need me?" she countered, flipping her long black hair back in a flirtatious manner. At least, she hoped the move was flirty.

"How does yesterday sound?" he quipped, tossing a towel onto his shoulder in a move it seemed like all bartenders had perfected. The man behind the bar was tall, a little better than six feet if she had to guess. He looked like he spent his days beside a swimming pool. His hair and eyes were dark, his smile friendly enough.

"My friend Liz Fox said this is a good place to work, so if you're serious about an opening, I'm game," she said, noticing how little recognition there was with the name.

He shrugged and then said, "You'd have to put up with me, but the pay is good." Then, his smile faded. "Seriously, though, what can I get you to drink?"

"No job then?" She figured there was no harm in being sure.

"Not today, sweetheart," he said, the condescending word bit right to the bone.

"I'll try next door then," she said, setting the cardboard mustache down on the bar and making a move to step away.

"I might not have a job for you, but I get off work in two hours if you want help figuring out where to apply next," he said with a wink that made her skin crawl.

"Thanks," she said, wishing she could step into a shower for how gross that statement made her feel. This guy needed to be punched in the face or at the very least slapped into the twenty-first century. He seemed like the kind of man who thought it was okay to pat any woman on the backside as she walked past or cat-call whistle from a distance.

Indignation wouldn't solve the mystery of Liz Fox or Military Cut, so Eileen cut her losses and headed toward the door. As she pushed through the throng of people, trying to make it to the door in one piece, a hand squeezed around her wrist. She whirled around to find a young female holding up a mustache against her face. All Eileen could make out was a pair of ocean-blue eyes before the crowd forced the two ladies away from each other.

A hand found hers and she felt a folded piece of paper being pressed into her palm. She fisted her hand and headed outside. A quick look back, she realized ocean eyes hadn't followed. It was a shame because Eileen still had so many questions and no answers. It had only been a little while since she'd shown at Lawson's place and yet in some ways an eternity had passed while she prayed for answers. First, to find out whether or not Kevin had been having an affair. Now, if he'd been a dirty cop to boot. None of this sat well. As much as she wanted to hate him for seeking out comfort from someone else, she couldn't. Although she didn't step outside of their marriage, it didn't long for her to fear she'd made a mistake. She didn't have the luxury to second guess any of it now because at the end of the day, he was still little Kevin's father. For his sake, she would figure out a way to forgive and move on. Besides, it wasn't like she could confront her husband about it and they weren't exactly trying to save a marriage. He was gone.

Outside on the busy street, she scanned the sidewalk and tucked the note inside the bottom of her purse. Anyone could be out here, watching, including Liz Fox or whatever her real name might be. Was she Ocean Eyes from inside the bar?

Eileen itched to read the message but didn't want to risk it right now. She could unfold the paper in the Jeep once she got back to Lawson. Besides, her heart threatened to batter her ribcage if she didn't find him. A couple of scenarios raced through her thoughts, none of them good. Had someone gotten to him while she was inside the bar? She wouldn't have heard a thing against the music and loud conversation. Panic gripped her thinking about the possibility something could have happened to him, to Kodo.

Hold on. There would be sirens if there'd been gunfire in downtown Austin. People would be freaking out. She tried to slow her breathing and think rationally again when she caught someone move across the street out of the corner of her eye. She looked and then squinted to see if she could make out the...Military Cut?

What was he doing here? Was Ocean Eyes trying to warn her about him? Was this his haunt?

Her mind snapped to Lawson and Kodo. She skimmed the street and saw they were crossing half a block away and heading toward Military Cut. She had no idea what her next move was supposed to be, so she tucked her chin to her chest and headed back the way she came. Military Cut fell back and out of sight. She didn't want to turn to look since he might not know she'd spotted him in the first place. Giving herself away seemed like a bad move, considering Lawson had locked onto Military Cut. She didn't want to draw suspicion, so she acted like she knew what she was doing. It dawned on her that she might not want to walk him straight to the Jeep. She could keep on this street for another block or two.

If nothing happened soon, she would duck into a restaurant or bar. There were plenty on this stretch of 5th Street to choose from. Just in the half block she'd walked so far, she'd passed several establishments.

The crowd was starting to thin out the farther she walked. Could she risk a glance at Military Cut?

Before she could turn, a man bolted down the opposite side of the street. Since several heads turned toward him, she looked too. Sure enough, Military Cut was on the run, and Lawson and Kodo were chasing him. Eileen stood there, spellbound by what was unfolding. There was no slack in Kodo's leash. For a half second, she wished Lawson would stop long enough to unhook his K9 partner. As Military Cut took a sharp right in the opposite direction, Lawson stopped long enough to find her. Instead of going after the guy, Lawson made a beeline for her despite what looked like Kodo's protests.

By the time he jogged over, both were breathing hard.

"Let's go," he said to her without an explanation. She followed him as he doubled back and then made the trek around the block to the Jeep. He didn't stop or slow down one bit until they were back at the vehicle. "I couldn't give chase."

"Why not? What happened?" she asked.

"He wasn't technically doing anything wrong. Kodo and I are law enforcement officers. There was no way I could unleash him, no matter how much we both wanted it," he explained. She noticed he was keeping Kodo at a safe distance from her. The dog looked keyed up. Would he bite?

Lawson opened the door and retrieved a bottle of water. He poured it out slowly, using his other hand as a makeshift bowl for Kodo to drink from. Lawson's gaze kept scanning the area, a constant reminder of the danger they were in.

Once Kodo hopped into the backseat, Lawson started the engine and turned on the A/C. He came around to the passenger door and then opened it for her before helping her inside. Next, he reclaimed the driver's seat.

"I got a message from someone inside the bar," Eileen said, digging into the bottom of her purse to locate the folded-up paper. She did. "This young woman placed it in my hand. I think she might have been a server or a barback, but I'm not certain."

"What does it say?" he asked, putting the gearshift

in reverse before backing out of the spot. He seemed like he couldn't get away from there fast enough.

She had to grab her phone for the flashlight app and then shined it on the page. *Leave. Fast.*

"Well, I think we've found the hangout," he said as he navigated onto the road.

"What do we do about it?"

"Good question." He thumped his flat palm against the steering wheel. "We were close tonight, though."

"What do you make of the guy you were chasing?" she asked, wondering what his take on Military Cut might be.

"He used to be either in the military or a cop, or both," he said. "He recognized me and Kodo almost right away, even though we were being casual." He paused. "Well, as casual as you can be with a trained K9 officer at your side."

"Kodo doesn't exactly look like a pet," she said to him.

"No, especially not to someone who has been around a K9 officer," he admitted.

"He might have given you away, but the guy still couldn't put the two of us together," she reasoned. "We weren't walking together or seen with one another. In fact, you came from a different direction altogether."

"Kodo and I were made by him," he said. "Now, the guy is going to realize the heat is on. He might not show up at the bar again for a while until things 'cool' off. He was a good trail to follow and now we have nothing."

"What if he tries to move faster now? What if he thinks I'm onto something?" she asked.

"Good points," he said. "He came out of the bar

from around the back seconds after you went in the front door."

"Which is strange because I've never seen him before up close. Not that I know of anyway and not while Kevin was alive." She searched her memory bank for the man and came up empty. "I can't help but wonder if the two were connected in some way."

"A phone call triggered this, right?" he asked.

"Yes," she stated.

"Maybe he was the guy on the other end of the line."

Hope was dangerous. And yet, it bubbled in her chest anyway. They were getting closer to the truth, closer to the answers she desperately needed. Rather than risk another huge letdown if this turned into a dead end, she shoved as much of the hope as she could somewhere down deep where it couldn't wreck her again like her marriage had.

CHAPTER TEN

Lawson turned over the events in his mind as he drove. A thought occurred to him that she might not be safe back at her house. By being run off the road, the situation was escalating. Plus, they were closer to his now that they were back in Austin. It was late and she was starting to look exhausted. "Do you want to stay at my place tonight?"

"I hate being so far away from little Kevin in case he needs me," she said honestly. "But I don't exactly want to go home either. It's too late to see if I can sleep over at Millie's in the guest room."

"You've stayed there before?" he asked, figuring they needed to talk about something besides the case. Any time he concentrated too hard on solving a problem, the answers seemed to run farther. Take a break, think of something else, or better yet try to get something accomplished and the problem seemed to solve itself.

He needed a direction now that they were in the

Jeep, so he headed toward home. At the very least, they needed to swing by and check on her vehicle.

"A few times when I first moved here. I left my old house so fast after Kevin died, that I hadn't really processed everything that had happened or how I was going to do this as a single parent. Millie found me sitting on the steps of the back porch of my rental home one day crying my eyes out, and invited me to supper that night," she explained. The thought of her suffering was a shot to his heart. Kevin's death had nearly gutted Lawson too. Everyone dealt with their emotions differently. He'd closed up and gone somewhere inside himself, not really talking to anyone about it. His workouts got a whole lot more intense. His guilt about not contacting Eileen to see how she was doing had been a weight on his chest that threatened to drag him to the ocean floor. Ignoring it didn't make it go away but seeing her seemed like it would only make everything harder. Now, he felt even worse. Her parents had essentially abandoned her after her sister's death, and he was no better. Granted, his attraction to Eileen had stopped him from picking up the phone every time he thought about her. He'd spent countless nights tossing and turning in bed trying to block her from his thoughts. He'd failed at that too.

"Millie sounds like the neighbor everyone needs," he said, ignoring the ache in his chest that had him wanting to reach out to Eileen and be her comfort. That path was dangerous. It had him wondering if he should stick around after the case was solved. To what end?

"She has been a godsend," she admitted. "I honestly don't know what I would have done without her."

"I'm glad you didn't have to find out." Heaven knew he hadn't been there for Eileen when she'd needed a friend the most. Despite the guilt threatening to consume him now, he took solace in the fact not everyone had let her down.

"Me too," she said. "She invited me to sleep in her guest room that night, after finding out that I was pregnant. It was still early, so I wasn't exactly showing yet. The movers literally dropped off the boxes, barely put my furniture together, and then bolted. So, I took her up on the guest room offer. One night turned into two. Suddenly, I'm there for five days and Millie knows my whole life story."

"I'm sorry for letting you down." It should have been him helping her move and get settled into the new place. The feeling he'd let Kevin down was an anchor that would drag him to the bottom of the ocean if he let it. But Lawson wasn't the only one who'd let her down. He couldn't begin to imagine what had been going through Kevin's mind. An affair? Dirty dealings? How could Lawson have missed the signs his friend was in trouble?

Easy. Lawson had made himself scarce after the wedding.

Once Kevin claimed Eileen, Lawson had had no choice but to back off. He went off to lick his wounds, while convincing himself that he was doing it for Kevin and Eileen, when in reality it was self-preservation. He'd known the second he laid eyes on Eileen from across the room that he was a goner. He wasn't ready and then he paid the price. To be fair, he'd had no idea that Kevin would want to date her. Although, he should have seen it. Eileen was not just the most beautiful person in every room. After talking to her for a few minutes, it was easy to see that she was intelligent. She was a little on the quiet side, but it didn't take much to coax her personality out.

"None of this was your fault," Eileen finally said after a long pause. "It's not mine, either. I blamed myself in the beginning too. Should I have asked more questions? Been a better wife? Would that have kept Kevin home?"

"You didn't do anything wrong," he said emphatically.

"Oh yeah? Then, neither did you."

He wasn't ready to let himself off the hook, so he didn't respond. She would only come up with another argument that he would be forced to let go in one ear and out the other.

"Do you mind if I stay at your place tonight?" she asked, catching him off guard with the question. "I think that's the best option all things considered. Plus, now that I think about it, I don't really want to go home."

"I'll have you back first thing in the morning," he promised before she could change her mind.

It would be nice if the investigation was official in some ways. Gaining access to resources topped the list. The problem was that Kevin's secret would be out if Lawson went through proper channels. Right now, they didn't have a viable threat to Eileen either. A handwritten note telling her to stay away from a bar wasn't exactly proof she was in danger. As far as the car running her off the road, she'd admitted the vehicle had swerved in front of her. She couldn't be certain the hit was intentional, and she hadn't stuck around to get a license plate so they could follow up. Austin drivers would be described as bad on a good day. A swerve wasn't akin to attempted assault or, worse yet, murder. Military Cut's identity was still an unknown. Then, he remembered the pictures he'd taken.

"I'm tired," she said before he could bring up the subject. "Mind if I lay my head back and rest?"

"Not at all," he said as she yawned. A few minutes of sleep could do Eileen a world of good. She'd bit back several yawns in the past few minutes, a sure sign her adrenaline spike was wearing off.

For the rest of the short ride, her eyes were closed and her breathing steady. He skipped checking on her vehicle since she was out most of the drive and parked in his usual spot on the pad beside his townhome. Kodo exited the Jeep the minute Lawson opened the driver's side door. Eileen didn't stir. Rather than disturb her, he jogged over and unlocked the door.

The thought people he cared about could be gone in the blink of an eye was another thing sitting heavy on his chest. He resolved to call his father in the morning. With everyone back at the ranch, Lawson found that he wanted to go home to Quinnland to visit if only to see how much life on the ranch had changed.

When he was at Eileen's earlier, he'd seen a picture of her newborn son on the nightstand. The kid was cute and small. He looked like a wise and wrinkled old man. Lawson couldn't help but think it was a shame the boy would grow up without a father. His mother had died when Lawson was too young to remember her. He'd always wondered how different his childhood might have been if she'd lived. What would it have been like to have a mother who volunteered at school or baked cookies for the fundraisers? What would it have been like to have feminine touches around the house instead of a father who ate in front of the TV on the times he was home for dinner? What would it have been like to be put to bed by his mother's touch when he'd been little?

Eileen's son deserved better. Lawson's blood boiled at the thought of Kevin cheating on her though. The e-mails were proof. There was no way Lawson would disrespect someone who was gone even though he couldn't help but wonder what kind of father Kevin would have been. Lawson had to believe his friend would have stepped up if Eileen would have been able to forgive him for the affair.

Lawson set those thoughts aside as he picked Eileen up. She barely stirred. Instead, she curled around him, wrapping her arms around his neck as he carried her into the townhouse. He walked her straight to the master bedroom that was located on the first floor, and then set her down as gently as he could. He slid her shoes off to make her more comfortable and wrapped the comforter around her.

He slipped out of the room, figuring he could sleep on the sofa if he needed to. He was thinking too hard about Kevin and letting emotions get in the way. After a few hours of sleep, he would brew a fresh pot of coffee and find a way to emotionally detach from the case. Come morning, he expected to start finding answers.

Lawson slipped into the shower and then got ready for bed without disturbing Eileen. As he tiptoed out of the room, he heard her shift position. She muttered something unintelligible. He forced himself to keep going when he wanted to climb in the bed beside her and be her comfort. She needed answers more than anything else, he reminded himself. Those would provide solace. She wouldn't get them if he didn't keep focused on what was important. He'd lost her to Kevin more than two years ago. No matter how strong the attraction was that brewed between them, nothing could come of it. His ego had been bruised when she'd moved on with Kevin so easily. What had he expected, though? He'd been the one to step aside.

And Kevin blew it, the annoying voice in the back of his mind said. Considering his friend was gone, it didn't seem right to point out the fact. But make no mistake about it, Kevin had ruined his marriage by cheating. Even if Eileen forgave him after she found out, and she would have figured it out at some point, there would have been no going back to the kind of trust she deserved.

Lawson had been cheated on once by a girlfriend. It had been game over for any future with her. Marriage was a different ballgame. He would take those vows seriously. As much as it wasn't his place to judge another person, he was ashamed of his friend for the affair. It wouldn't matter if Kevin had married someone Lawson had never met, he would still shake his head. Why his friend didn't come to him with concerns, he'd never know.

Then again, Lawson had pulled back from their friendship after Kevin started dating Eileen. He'd withdrawn based on the excuse he was giving a new couple time to get to know each other. In truth, he'd been protecting his own heart. So, yeah, he couldn't escape part of the blame. If he'd been there for Kevin, maybe he could have talked him out of the mysterious Liz Fox.

The annoying voice in the back of his mind that was usually right picked that moment to pipe in. *Kevin didn't have to have an affair. He could have come to you.*

As much as Lawson might agree, he still should have been there for his friend. Kevin must have been drowning with all the new responsibility. The guy didn't normally stick around much after the first few dates. The shine wore off his new relationships faster than a salesmen's dress shoes. Sticking around, making the ultimate commitment, and then learning about a pregnancy must have been foreign territory to Kevin.

If Lawson hadn't been too busy licking his wounds, he might have seen his friend drowning. So, yeah, he felt like a class-A jerk for letting Kevin down and for dropping the ball with Eileen too. He would have gone back and done anything to save her from the pain even if it meant sacrificing any chance with her all over again.

The realization smacked him in the face because the idea behind it went far deeper than friendship or loyalty. It sounded a whole lot like love.

Eileen blinked her eyes open and immediately sat up the moment she realized she was in unfamiliar surroundings. She should probably be panicked right now, except there was a familiar and comforting scent wrapping around her as she breathed in. Lawson.

As she got her bearings, she realized she was in his bed, underneath his comforter. Made sense why his unique scent was all over her. She pushed aside the thought that she could get used to this because it felt a lot like home.

A bathroom was adjacent, so she went in and cleaned herself up. A toothbrush was sitting on the counter still in its wrapper along with a tube of toothpaste. There were other necessities too. She washed up and then headed into the main living area.

The sun was already up. A quick glance over at the clock said it was half past seven in the morning. She'd slept a long time. Much longer than usual, especially since little Kevin came along. Speaking of him, she needed to check in with Millie. Her and the baby would be up by now.

"Morning," Lawson said. His deep timbre washing over her wasn't something she was ready to deal with first thing and without caffeine. If sex had a voice, it would be the gravelly sound of his in the morning.

"Morning," she parroted, making a beeline for the coffee machine, thankful the smell of a fresh pot overpowered his masculine scent.

After pouring a fresh cup and taking a couple of sips, she located her cell. The battery was low. She bit back a curse. Of course, it was. She forgot to bring a charger. She must have been frowning because Lawson responded.

"Everything okay over there?" he asked.

She held up her cell phone. "Battery."

"Charger is on the counter over there." He pointed to a spot at the end of the granite counter where the kitchen ended and the breakfast room began. There was a small table that would fit four comfortably in the nook.

"Thank you," she said, palming her coffee in one hand and her cell in the other. She had to set down the black roast in order to plug in her phone. After picking up the cup and taking another sip, she made the call.

"Hello." Millie answered on the first ring.

"How's my baby today?" she immediately asked.

"An angel, like usual," Millie's voice practically sang when she talked about little Kevin. It made Eileen's heart do the same.

"He slept well then," she said.

"Didn't wake up once, not even when you got back," Millie said.

Hold on a second.

"I'm not back," Eileen clarified.

"Really?" Millie sounded confused as Eileen spun around to face Lawson, who'd perked up considerably after hearing the tone in Eileen's voice.

"No," Eileen confirmed.

"I could have sworn that I heard you come in around four o'clock in the morning," she said. "Might be raccoons in the trash again."

"Maybe," Eileen said, concerned it might be Military

Cut from the bar last night. She didn't want to explain why it might have been a person since that would definitely freak Millie out. Riling her up for no reason didn't seem like a good idea. "Or some other kind of animal."

"We get all kinds of critters out here. Could have sworn I heard a vehicle, though," she said on a sigh. "Oh well, at my age I confuse things all the time. Might have been my imagination."

Eileen highly doubted it. She also wanted to get home to see if anything was missing. The boxes were out in her bedroom, opened. It would be easy to slip in and take whatever someone wanted. Would it be smart to warn Millie? It couldn't hurt to have the older woman watching her back.

"Be careful, okay?" she asked.

"I've got Sampson if anyone wants to come snooping around over here," she quipped. Sampson was the shotgun that her husband bought for protection when he had to leave for two days at a time to buy specialty plants from growers around the state. They were small operations that had no delivery system back in the day. Times had changed and so had shipping. Even so, Eileen planned to pick up those visits as soon as little Kevin was old enough to go more than a few hours without a meal. She loved the idea of finding specialty plants no one else had in stock. Plus, Millie's Plant Shack was known for going the extra mile for its customers. Millie admitted to letting that slip since losing her husband. Eileen wanted to bring the Plant Shack back to its former glory. She wanted to do Millie—the woman who'd become a second mother to her—proud.

"Keep him close, okay?" she said by way of warning.

"Anything specific I need to be concerned about?" Millie had a way of getting to the bottom of a situation.

"General warning," Eileen said, figuring the threat was aimed at her and not her neighbor. Still, she didn't want to risk Millie getting caught in the crossfire.

"Got it," she said.

The sounds of her son working up a fuss in the background had Millie needing to go.

"Let me know when you come home and I'll bring him over for a spell to say hello," Millie said.

"Better wait for me to come there," Eileen stammered, trying to come up with an excuse on the fly. "I would just rather get in and get out of my house with the boxes that need to go. I'm already an emotional wreck, and I don't feel good about little Kevin seeing me this way."

"Babies do pick up on moods," Millie agreed, but there was a note of caution in her voice Eileen hadn't heard before. She seemed to shake it off when she said, "Stop by whenever. We'll be here or in the garden." Then she added, "With Sampson nearby."

CHAPTER ELEVEN

"What did she see?" Lawson sat up and gripped his coffee mug. He was ready to bolt in a heartbeat if needed. He'd been up almost the entire night trying to figure out a connection between Military Cut, Liz Fox, and a note that read: *Leave. Fast.*

Of course, he wanted to drive right back to the bar tonight when it opened and ask a whole lot of questions. All the answers pointed toward the bar. He'd shot a note to one of his buddies at work, asking if there were any unofficial rumors circulating about the Mustache Bar. When Jacob Myer asked what the deal was, Lawson said he went downtown with a date and left with a bad feeling about the place. He was still waiting for a response.

"First of all, sorry I fell asleep last night on the way home," Eileen joined him in the living room where he had Kevin's laptop. Thankfully, he'd thought to bring it last night if there'd been an intruder. "In all the excitement of Military Cut and the note from the random waitress, I forgot to tell you the bartender was no help and ended our conversation by hitting on me."

Lawson had to stop himself from popping off at the mouth as to what the bartender could do with his libido. He white-knuckled the coffee mug as Kodo's ears perked up. He stood up and headed straight for the front door.

Was someone out there? Setting down his cup, he put a hand up to essentially tell Eileen not to move. If someone was trying to peek in a window, he didn't want her drawing attention to herself. She was far enough away in the kitchen to be blocked from a couple of the windows.

Kodo took Lawson's actions as a green light to investigate. He went right to the door as he listened. Then, he moved to the closest window before pacing back. Lawson located his service weapon. Back against the wall, he moved around to the opposite side of the room.

A low growl tore from Kodo's throat as Lawson moved to a window and peeked in between the blinds. "Delivery."

He gave Kodo the command to stand down, before returning his Glock to the holster hanging in the coat closet. The sounds of a vehicle pulling away confirmed the driver was gone. Lawson moved to the front door and then opened it. A package sat on the small porch. He remembered ordering a new charger for his cell phone. One he could take with him and plug in as many devices as necessary.

Grabbing the small package, he headed back in the

house to two pairs of eyes on him. He held up the box. "Charger. The kind that speed charges."

"I need to get one of those," Eileen said, but the tension in her body was still visible.

He set the item on top of his coffee table. "You were going to tell me about your conversation with Millie."

"Oh. Right." She shook her head as if to shake off the stress. "She was convinced we came home last night. Heard a vehicle and everything."

"What time?" he asked.

"Around four a.m.," she said.

"A couple of hours after our visit to the bar." He didn't like it. The note from the server was a head scratcher. The first word made sense. *Leave.* She was telling Eileen to get out of there. The second word was the part he couldn't figure out. *Fast.* What did it mean? Why capitalize the word and use punctuation?

"That's right," Eileen said. "I thought about that too. And the message from the server."

"Too bad we don't have a picture of the woman," he said, not wanting to spell out the name of Kevin's mistress.

Fast. He repeated the word a couple more times with the same result...nothing. It didn't ring any bells or make sense. Not to him. They couldn't exactly waltz back in the bar tonight and flag down the waitress.

"She held up a mustache," Eileen said. She must be thinking along the same lines as him. "I couldn't get a good look at her face but took note of ocean blue eyes. Then, she was gone and I was being pushed in the opposite direction."

Eileen brought her hand up to cover a gasp.

"You don't think she's in any sort of trouble for slipping me that note, do you?" she asked.

He picked up his cell phone. "I'll shoot a note to one of my buddies to see if there were any domestic abuse cases or homicides downtown involving female victims." He fired off a text and noticed a response to his earlier text was there waiting. He'd placed his cell on silent so it wouldn't disrupt Eileen's rest. He'd kept the door open to the master bedroom, so he could hear her stirring from down the hall. The last thing he wanted was her waking up in a stranger's bed in an unfamiliar home. The door wasn't visible from the living room, so she was able to keep her privacy. The urge to check on her had been strong. There were too many temptations sleeping in his bed last night. He'd steered clear while keeping watch.

"There has been suspicious activity around the Mustache Bar since a new owner took over two years ago," he said as he read the text from his buddy Jacob. The place wasn't on Lawson's beat, but it was on his friend's.

"Sounds like no one has been able to make a direct tie to any crime ring," she said.

"Nope. Not according to my friend Jacob."

"I know him," Eileen stated. The statement caught him off guard even though it shouldn't. She would have known or at least heard of some of the other guys on the force. "You know, I don't think Kevin ever really liked him."

"Did he mention anything specifically?" he asked, confused by her statement considering the three of them had been friends.

She shook her head. "Just a feeling I got."

"Was it always like that?" he asked.

"In the time I knew him...yes," she confirmed.

"I wonder when they grew apart," he said, realizing that for someone who was supposed to be so observant, he'd missed the boat on some of the people closest to him. "We all used to be buddies at one time. I guess we all went our separate ways but the two of them used to still get together occasionally."

"They would hang out in the garage sometimes after work when..." She flashed eyes at him like she didn't want to say something that might hurt his feelings.

He cocked an eyebrow and held his tongue.

"When you stopped coming over."

"Was there a definitive time that you remember Kevin and Jacob cutting off their friendship?" he asked, not liking the direction of this conversation at all.

"Not really," she said. "I guess I was so tired with the pregnancy and sick in the early weeks that everything else faded into the background. Kevin was gone a lot and when he wasn't..." She shrugged. "I guess I didn't notice as much. My focus went to getting enough rest. I thought...*hoped*...he'd come around to the marriage and be happy at some point but the pregnancy only made it worse."

She didn't specifically say that she'd become disillusioned with the marriage but the notion hung in the air.

"You were dealing with a surprise pregnancy too," he pointed out, hoping she wasn't too hard on herself about the marriage being what it was.

She nodded.

"He should have stepped up, Eileen."

"I know," was all she seemed able to say about the situation. She had to have had the breath knocked out of her then and again now after finding out about the affair.

"For what it's worth," he began, "I know he loved you."

"Love is a funny word for what we shared," she said after a thoughtful pause. "Love, to me at least, is being there for each other when the chips are down. It's being side-by-side during life's biggest challenges and sweetest moments. It's supporting each other and lifting each other up, not tearing each other down."

He had no excuses to offer for his friend. Kevin's cheating was wrong in every sense of the word. She made a whole lot of good points—points he would probably be making if his relationship had fallen apart at the seams in a similar manner.

She waved a hand in the air and then coughed. He instantly knew she was covering the fact she was working up to tears.

"I'm sorry he treated you that way," Lawson said. "Truly sorry. He had no right in a marriage to step out on you. Before that, he had no right to ask me to step aside if all he was going to do was abandon you when you needed him the most. The pregnancy had to have scared you too, but you didn't react the same way. You didn't run away or hide behind an affair. He never should have put you through what he did. You shouldn't have had to go through the pregnancy alone. And he shouldn't have brought danger to your doorstep."

She quietly shook her head while keeping her gaze

steady on the tile flooring underneath her feet like if she looked up, she might start crying.

"I'm sorry for the way Kevin treated you," he said a little louder this time. "He's gone now and you're left cleaning up the mess. I don't know what he got himself into, but I plan to see this through to the end. You don't have to figure this out alone, Eileen." He stopped short of saying he should have stepped up when they'd first met, instead of stepping aside when Kevin made his move. He should have realized that Kevin would have become restless once she fell for him. The guy hadn't had a relationship that lasted more than a month since Lawson had met him. Maybe that was the reason he'd stepped aside when Kevin had asked. Not in a million years had Lawson believed Kevin would have stuck with a relationship more than a month. He certainly hadn't guessed his friend would propose. But then, what had he believed would happen? Kevin and Eileen would date. He would get bored and move on. Then what?

Lawson's words, his kindness touched Eileen in a very deep place. The weight of anger and shame lifted, and she could breathe again. There was so much she wanted to say in response. None of it seemed adequate in expressing how she felt in that moment. The word *free* came to mind, but it wasn't quite right. *Light* was a little better. There was a lightness to her that she hadn't felt in too long.

And she was tired of sitting around and waiting for someone else to decide the next move.

She'd waited for Lawson to step in that first night, and Kevin had instead. Rather than going for what she really wanted, she'd taken what was offered. If Lawson had known how much she'd wanted to be with him before, would he have reacted the same? After losing Kevin, she thought a whole lot about time. How it gave to some and took away from others randomly. Literally, a person she loved could be gone in the snap of a finger. No warning. No time to work out problems or make things right. The past year or so had taught her that all she could ever really count on was this moment, the present. There were no guarantees, except everyone's life had an expiration date. She held onto the belief there was something out there, something better, something worth going to when this life was done. But all she really knew for certain was that tomorrow was guaranteed no one.

When she thought about it in those terms, wasting time seemed like the worst offense of all. Sitting around, waiting for someone else to act, made very little sense to her when she was in this mood.

Deciding to act on what *she* really wanted for a change, she walked over to Lawson and pressed a kiss to his thick, full lips. He brought his hands up to cup her face. His touch was a strange mix of electricity and comfort. Heat enveloped her when the kiss meant to be a peck quickly morphed into so much more.

Thunder clapped overhead, another storm on the way. More rain. All she could think was how much the earth needed rain for nourishment. Very few things grew in dry soil. A tear welled in her eye and then spilled down her cheek. Being this close to Lawson, touching and kissing, could bring on a downpour.

This time, she was the first one to pull back. Neither mentioned regrets either or whether or not what they'd just done was smart. He seemed as mesmerized by the moment happening between them as she'd been.

"Thank you," she said low and under her breath. Those words covered so many things, not the least of which was the sense of rightness he brought back to her world when it had been turned upside down. Upside down and still spinning.

After a couple of deep breaths, she moved back into the kitchen and refilled her coffee cup. The dark roast flavor had tasted so much better on Lawson's lips after he'd had a cup, but this would have to do. "Whenever you're ready to head out, we should swing by my place and see if anything's missing."

"Okay," he said, and his voice was still more than a little gravelly. They made eye contact that lingered a little longer than was probably safe. The world slowed down for just a moment, and they were the only two people on earth.

"I'll grab my purse," she finally said. She was relieved he was having the same physical reaction after they touched as she was. Her body wanted more, and it took a minute or two to find the strength to reset. Coffee gave her something else to focus on.

"You should eat something before we head out," he said, pushing up to standing. "Cereal all right?"

"Fine with me," she said, noticing she was hungrier than she realized.

Eileen took note of how nice it was for someone to take care of her. She was perfectly capable of caring for herself. She didn't need anyone to hold her hand and yet there was something incredible and wonderful about having someone to lean on. She wasn't accustomed to the feeling, having always been forced to do for herself.

This seemed like a good time to remind herself not to get too used to it.

After a quick bowl of Cheerios, while Kodo ate next to them, the trio headed out to the Jeep.

"I can't seem to shake the feeling that the message from the waitress last night meant more than we realize," Lawson stated, after giving Kodo a minute to take care of business.

"Something has been niggling at the back of my mind too," she admitted. "I just wish I knew what."

"Maybe we'll get answers at your place," he said.

"We can only hope."

CHAPTER TWELVE

Traffic on the drive to Eileen's home wasn't bad that morning. They made good time and polished off another coffee in the process as she seemed to sit on the edge of the passenger seat. The second Lawson put the gearshift in park, she bolted out of the vehicle.

"Hold on a second," he warned, racing to catch up to her before she made it halfway across the lawn with Kodo at his side. He'd parked on the street rather than pull up right next to her house on the off chance someone was still inside. "We don't know what we're walking into."

Eileen gasped as she turned to face him. Eyes wide, it seemed to dawn on her they might not be alone.

"You mentioned something about wanting to see little Kevin this morning. How about this, I'll check the perimeter and secure your home while you run next door and visit?" he asked, figuring it was the best way to keep her safe while he cleared the place.

"Are you sure you'll be all right by yourself?" she

asked, and then seemed to catch herself as she glanced down at Kodo.

"We're good," he said with a wink.

"Okay. That's probably a good idea," she said before taking a few slow, deep breaths most likely meant to calm her. Before heading over, she pushed up to her tiptoes and kissed him again before handing over her house keys. He could get used to this, even though he warned himself not to.

"I'll text you when it's safe to come back," he said, drawing his weapon.

"Okay," she said, before heading toward Millie's.

With the sun out and it being broad daylight, he could watch to make sure she made it inside safely. The threat of rain had passed, and it was shaping up to be a nice day. This time of year, anything could happen from freezing rain to flip-flop weather. Personally, he was more of a boot guy, a habit from his childhood no doubt.

Eileen made it safely onto her neighbor's porch. She turned and waved, and it was like a bolt of stray lightning struck the center of his chest. Lawson was in trouble when it came to Eileen. She was exactly the kind of person he could see himself settling down with long-term. Being with her reminded him of all the good to be found in relationships. There'd never been a connection between two people like the one he felt with her. It was a mix of excitement and comfort, like he'd finally found home and couldn't wait to spend more time there. In fact, it was the only place he wanted to be.

Their attraction might be mutual, but their lives were complicated.

He gave the command for Kodo to work beside him. His partner cooperated, sniffing around the perimeter of the home. Since there had been rain recently, the soil was still moist. Lawson picked up on a large-sized running shoe imprint. In fact, the wearer had circled the house. Was he looking for an entry point?

Careful not to cover the tracks, Lawson followed the trail to where a vehicle must have been parked thirty feet from the home. There were tire tracks that definitely didn't belong to the Jeep. He thought about Eileen's vehicle and realized he didn't know what she drove. Her car was still parked near his home. They needed to retrieve it and park it in a safe place.

Lawson circled the bungalow one more time. There were no broken windows or signs of distress on the sills. The front door was still locked. He went around to the back and realized someone had forgotten to lock it when they left. He'd watched Eileen double-check the back door before they headed out to the bar last night, so he knew for certain it hadn't been her. Did Millie have a key? It could explain why the door was left unlocked. She might have come over to get one of the toys or supplies for the baby. With her hands full, she might have forgotten to lock the back door when she left.

He fished out his cell phone and fired off the question to Eileen. She was there with Millie so it would be easy enough to ask.

Leave. Fast. Those words kept cycling around in his thoughts. What did they have to do with each other?

Or did they? He was clearly looking at this wrong otherwise it would make sense.

Kevin was having an affair with Liz Fox. Was Military Cut her husband? If so, why would he be following Eileen? It was possible he'd found out about the affair, so when Eileen called the number, he might have believed his wife's lover was on the line instead. When she didn't speak, he might have gotten suspicious. How ridiculous would it be if all this could be cleared up over a beer?

The likelihood of that happening was slim to none after the road incident. Why not confront Eileen? Why not clear up the questions easily? Why leave the bar, going out the back door when she walked inside?

It didn't add up to a man being cheated on by his spouse. Kevin was a cop. Was it possible he'd been targeted from the get-go? A good way to blackmail him would be to have his mistress threaten to come forward and talk to his pregnant wife just as he had been threatened in the e-mails. Bringing the affair to light would destroy his reputation too. How far would Kevin go to keep the affair a secret? He'd met in person rather than hash the situation out over e-mails. Then, he'd been killed days later.

Lawson didn't like this line of thinking one bit. The two had never been partners, so he couldn't speak to the man's work history. As far as he knew Kevin was a respected officer. Despite being somewhat of a known flirt, he appeared to take his relationship with Eileen seriously. The term *looks could be deceiving* came to mind. Being an objective investigator when a friend was involved wasn't something Lawson took lightly. He had to follow the evidence just like any other case.

On the other hand, he wasn't a robot. He was mad as hell at Kevin for cheating. No one deserved to have that done to them, especially not someone as loyal and kind-hearted as Eileen. Setting aside his frustration, Lawson examined the backdoor. Lock picking tools were easy to come by and even easier to use. He suspected someone used one here if the Millie angle didn't pan out.

A couple of minutes had passed since he'd sent the text to Eileen. Shouldn't she be responding by now?

He double-checked his phone. Nothing had come through. He moved to the window and looked at Millie's house. There were no signs of distress. There'd been no screams. Still, his pulse kicked up a couple of notches.

Texts weren't always reliable. They didn't always go through. He pulled up her name in his contacts as Kodo sniffed around.

Eileen picked up on the second ring. "Everything okay?"

Hearing her voice calmed his racing pulse enough to breathe again. "All good here. Can you ask Millie if she stopped by after we left last night?"

"Sure." She relayed the question before coming back on the line. "No. She hasn't been over."

"Is she one hundred percent certain about that?" he pressed. The question would give away the fact there'd been someone in the house but he needed Millie to be sure. He couldn't count the number of times witnesses recanted a statement later in an investigation.

"I'll ask her again," Eileen said. The raised octave signaled that she was concerned. She repeated the question and he heard Millie's response. Eileen came back on the line. "She is one hundred percent certain that she's been here since she left my place last night." He waited for the inevitable question. "Why?"

"Someone has been here. The person circled the house, no doubt casing the place to make sure no one was home," he said.

"A safe assumption since my car is still parked over by your place," she stated.

"I thought the same thing," he agreed. "They came in through the backdoor. There are no signs of forced entry, so my guess is the person used a tool."

"It's that easy?" she asked.

"With a standard lock it is," he explained. "This is a small town compared to Austin, so most folks leave their doors unlocked. The person who showed up here had to have suspected you would have locked yours."

"Military Cut?"

"That's where my money is," he agreed.

"I'll be right over."

A shiver rocked Eileen's body as she tried to wipe away the image of a stranger breaking in through the back door, then walking around her home like he owned the place. She'd found this house on her own, spent her own money on it, and was doing her best to make it into a home for her and little Kevin. The icy chill she'd initially experienced was replaced by white-hot anger.

No one had the right to violate these walls. She might be renting but this was where she'd brought her newborn home to, and it would always hold a special place in her heart because of it. She'd come through that same door after parking in the back, cradling a helpless little infant and promising to do her best as a mother. Role models had been in short supply so she'd read every book she could get her hands on. Nothing prepared her for the kind of love she experienced when her little bundle was placed in her arms moments after he'd taken his first breath.

"What's going on inside your head right now?" Lawson asked the minute she entered through the back door.

"This isn't right. I feel violated and angry." She shook her head as though it might help her shake off the frustration. It helped a little.

He nodded. He probably had counseled dozens of people through similar situations, and yet he didn't try to throw words at her to make her feel better. He seemed to realize that she was going to have to process this in her own way, and she appreciated that. No words would make this feeling go away. She glanced down and realized she'd fisted her hands like she was gearing up for a fight.

"I need answers," was all she managed to say.

"Let's go into the bedroom and see if we can find some in the boxes," he said, Kodo at his heels.

She would probably be a whole lot more afraid without the two of them beside her. Between Lawson and Kodo, she had enough protection by her side. "There's no chance the person is still here, right?"

"No," he said, shaking his head. "Kodo would have found them by now."

"How does he do that?" she asked.

"He can smell adrenaline and fear. That's what he goes after when we don't have another scent to work with," he explained, as they walked side-by-side into the adjacent living room.

Before heading into the bedroom, they checked the laundry room, common areas, and baby's room. So far, nothing was out of place. But whoever had been here wasn't exactly trying to steal diapers and formula. What had Kevin done? It was one thing to have an affair. That was bad enough. But to get involved in something illegal in the process? Clearly, his head wasn't on straight and she couldn't even venture a guess as to what he'd gotten himself into that could spill over once he was gone. If only she'd let a sleeping dog lie and hadn't felt the need to call that number, her and little Kevin's lives would look very different right now.

Then again, if that hadn't happened, she wouldn't have had a reason to contact Lawson. Whatever else was happening between them, she realized she could count on him as a friend to lean on. Little Kevin could use all the positive male role models he could get. Lawson fit that bill one hundred percent.

Thinking back to the honky tonk bar, she'd never asked Lawson why he'd stepped aside. It wouldn't even occur to her now except that she felt the chemistry between them. She'd felt the same sizzle when they'd first laid eyes on each other. Why did he back off?

The easy answer was that he just wasn't that into her. Keeping her guard up was probably a good idea.

Right now, Lawson had mixed emotions. He'd lost a friend, found out said friend had treated her wrong, and the same friend was also involved in something illegal. It had to be. There was no other explanation for Military Cut showing up like this otherwise.

This seemed like a good time to remind herself to be careful with her heart. Having a baby had only made it softer and more vulnerable. Losing someone like Lawson after she let him in would shatter her. She'd already lost Kevin, a man she'd let herself love in the early days of their relationship. Strange how different the two emotions felt when it came to Kevin and Lawson. Then again, her radar came up early in her marriage. It was almost like being a bird and having her wings clipped moments after she'd learned to fly. She'd gone into protective mode as she'd spiraled to the ground.

Having her son was making her see how many different shapes and sizes love came in. Only a rare few could touch her as deeply as little Kevin, and now Lawson, did. Exactly the reason she needed to get a tighter grip on her emotions toward Lawson. She could do friendship and she could use someone to lean on. But letting herself go down the full path was like lighting herself on fire and hoping she wouldn't get burned.

"Does anything look out of place? Rummaged through?" he asked, breaking into her thoughts with that whiskey-soaked voice of his.

After opening and closing a few drawers in each room, she said, "Nothing looks out of place. I do tend to throw things in drawers and shut them, so they are usually a mess. I'm not sure I would notice if someone had gone through them looking for something or not."

"None of the drawers were left partially open. Whoever was here would have most likely been in a hurry," he deduced. His experience would give him a better leg to stand on when talking about what might have happened. "There should be some signs a person was here."

"They had to be coming for what was in the boxes," she said. "I didn't exactly take inventory so I would have no idea if something was missing."

"We already had the laptop and phone, which would be my guess as to why someone would break in but maybe that's too obvious," he stated, while looking around for what she figured was other obvious signs of rummaging.

"It's a good thing we took those," she said. "I'd stuffed the boxes in the back of the closet when I moved here because I couldn't face opening them right away."

"Someone might have been here before to check the place out," he said. "With the boxes hidden out of sight, the perp might have slipped in and slipped out sight unseen."

"Doesn't that thought make me want to throw up a little," she said with a shiver.

"People should feel safe in their own homes," he stated. "Last night, taking the laptop and cell phone with us probably saved those items from being stolen. I can dig around to see if there's more than just the hidden e-mail account."

"How did you find that, by the way?" she asked. "The e-mail?"

"It's not hard when you know what to look for and where to search it out," he explained. "A tech friend of mine told me how to do it and where to look."

"Can the same thing be possible on the phone?" she continued. "Hiding an app that has another e-mail on it?"

"Anything can be hidden but I doubt Kevin would put anything on his cell phone that might incriminate him," he said.

"Does that mean we're going back to the bar later today?" she asked, figuring it was the only place they'd gotten any sense of a direction.

"I don't see another choice," he stated. "But I don't like the risks."

"You can't stick by my side forever, Lawson," she said. "We're no further now than we were yesterday, when this all started going down. For all we know, I'm already in danger."

Could the person have gotten what they came for? When would she be safe to go home to little Kevin?

"I don't like the idea of poking the bear," he said. "Not when your life is on the line."

"You'll be around, and so will Kodo," she said with a confidence she didn't feel.

"I hope we're enough," he said quietly.

CHAPTER THIRTEEN

"I don't see anything out of place," Eileen said as she took a final lap around the bedroom. The fact there was a bed within a stone's toss from them wasn't lost on Lawson. The temptation to give in to the attraction sizzling between them was a simmering burn low in his belly. There wasn't a whole lot stopping them from doing the exact thing both seemed to want more than air at times. They had time to kill and no one else around to stop them.

The question wasn't whether or not they both wanted to have sex that was guaranteed to be the best in his life. The question was whether or not they could recover from it afterward and go back to their normal lives. Sex would change everything, and he knew on instinct once would never be enough.

What did that mean in the long run? They were just beginning a friendship. Would sex ruin it before it gained its footing?

"Okay," he said, hearing the gruff quality to his own voice. He cleared his throat.

"Nothing appears to be missing." She threw her hands in the air. "I have no idea what might have been taken from the boxes."

"Let's clean this up and secure the boxes in case the perp returns," Lawson said as Kodo found a spot in the doorway to sit, his protective instincts on full alert.

"The thought of someone being here once is bad enough," Eileen said on a visible shudder. "Do you really think they'll come back?"

"If they didn't get what they were looking for, they might," he reasoned. Up to this point, the perp had been avoiding Eileen. Stalking, yes, but slipping in when she was gone, rather than confronting her, was a good sign in an awful situation. He thought about how Military Cut had slipped out the back door of the bar. Was he concerned she would recognize him?

It was the only logical explanation. He must have been around here at some point or the home she'd shared with her husband. Someone must know something or spoke to Kevin at some point. Lawson's thoughts shifted back to Jacob.

Lawson pulled out his cell phone and fired off a text. *Can U talk?*

The three dots indicating a response was being typed showed up on the screen. They disappeared but no message came through. Strange. Lawson waited. A couple of minutes ticked by as he and Eileen closed up the boxes and then shoved them inside the back of the closet.

A couple of minutes passed before the dots returned. They disappeared almost as fast. No message.

Lawson decided to send another text. *OK?*

The lines appeared again. This time, a text came through a few seconds later. *Just u?*

Lawson cocked his head to one side. How did Jacob know Lawson was with Eileen? The two hadn't been together for long. Word couldn't have gotten out that fast. Could it?

Sure. Lawson's response was met with a thumb's up. He sent the next one. *Where?*

Jacob provided the address of a coffee shop in downtown Austin near 5th Street, not far from the bar. Interesting. Lawson gave a thumb's up to the text.

An hour? He wanted to meet soon to capitalize on the moment. He was concerned that if he said, *boo,* Jacob might ghost the meeting. The thumbs up sign came almost immediately. Good. It would take forty-five minutes to get there, giving him fifteen minutes to finish up here and update Eileen.

"Can I go with you?" she asked almost immediately.

"Yes, but it might be best if he doesn't see you. Instead of going into the coffee shop, you could maybe walk around the block, or I could park a few streets away and you could wait in the Jeep with Kodo." There was absolutely no way he was leaving her without protection downtown. He needed her as close as possible at all times to ensure her safety. Plus, there was a growing piece of him that couldn't stand the thought of being separated from her. He was going to have to deal with it once they cracked this mystery, but fully intended to put it off as long as possible.

Besides, he needed a minute to think about what she meant to him now, that she'd shown up in his life again. That was a discussion for later.

"I wish I could go with you, to hear what Jacob has to say firsthand," she said. "There's something about this whole setup that I don't trust."

"Exactly the reason I'd like you to be near me at all times," he said. "As we dig around, we are likely to make someone very uncomfortable and that could mean the person will become desperate. Desperate times can breed desperate actions."

"Okay," she seemed to agree with him, and he was struck by how much he wanted her with him. Not just to protect her, but also just because he liked having her around. He breathed better when she was in the room and his pulse calmed to a reasonable level. He would tell himself it was because of the danger she faced but there was so much more to it than that. On the most basic, primal level, he needed her.

It was good they were on the same page when it came to staying together to say the least. He rounded to the back door and then locked it.

"Let's head out the front," he said. Kodo took the lead. He picked up a scent leading out to a small garden shed. They'd checked the perimeter of the house and pretty much every inch of the place. No one had gone to the shed that he knew of.

Lawson called his dog back. Kodo kept going. The scent must be strong for him to be so locked onto it. Lawson whistled. Loud. Kodo's ears tilted toward his handler. Thankfully, he turned tail and came running back.

Nothing about this scenario felt good, so Lawson had Kodo follow him to the Jeep. He turned on the engine and gave the command for Kodo to hop into the backseat. He did but was still distracted by whatever was over near the garden shed.

Without speaking, Lawson nodded toward the Jeep. Eileen locked gazes before heading into the vehicle and the passenger seat. She climbed inside and closed the door as Lawson drew his weapon.

With his Sig leading the way, he moved one careful step at a time toward the shed. As he got close, he realized the door was ajar. Had the perp been searching inside there for something? This didn't feel right. Something was off. The hairs on the back of his neck pricked.

Years of experience combined with gut instincts told him to listen to those feelings when he got them. There was something going on with the concrete square in front of the door. Did he dare get close enough to get a good look? Was it some kind of trap?

He glanced around, checking the area. There were a few trees on the back and east side of the shed in between the houses. A shooter could be stationed there. But why? Why not use the same vantage point to shoot them as they walked inside the house?

The perp might use the spot to watch the home. Lawson moved over to the trees and saw there were tracks there too. So, someone had been watching her from the trees recently. He imagined the person had visited this spot often. The recent rain was the reason for the tracks showing up now. He didn't like the scenarios playing out in his thoughts.

A glance over at the Jeep and he saw that Kodo was

agitated. He was pacing back and forth in the backseat. Eileen seemed to be handling the situation. She waved him over. The shed could wait.

Lawson dropped the barrel of his gun toward the ground and then walked over, scanning the area for any signs of trouble. He wondered how safe it was for Millie and little Kevin at this point.

Setting the thought aside for now, he approached the Jeep. Kodo was clearly agitated.

The helpless look on Eileen's face nearly gutted Lawson. Her concern for Kodo warmed his heart. Kodo was one of the rare police dogs that could be trusted to be alone in a vehicle with her. But then, Kodo was a rare animal.

"Open the door," Lawson said to her, holding his weapon down toward the earth. She did. Kodo bolted out the door and straight toward the shed.

The bad feeling from a minute ago was like an anchor around Lawson's shoulders as he careened down toward the ocean floor. Something deep inside him told him to find a way to make Kodo stop. He shouted the command, then whistled. Neither of the tricks worked.

Lawson located a large rock the size of a baseball and threw it at the shed to get Kodo's attention, as he had already crossed half of the yard in a dead run. The next few seconds slowed to a crawl as an explosion blew the doors off the garden shed. Kodo jumped before landing on his front paws. He stumbled and then dropped to the ground as Lawson bit back a curse and ran to his partner.

On autopilot, he probably yelled for Eileen to call 911 even though his actions at this point were a blur.

Kodo lie on his side, panting, which was not a good sign. Anger ripped through Lawson at the possibility his partner was seriously injured. All he could think about was getting his hands on the person responsible and ensuring the perp spent a lifetime behind bars.

Kodo's rapid breathing meant he was in pain. Lawson wouldn't normally run to the officer down but the area had been cleared already, and there was no stopping him from assessing Kodo's condition.

"Where does it hurt?" he asked, knowing full well Kodo couldn't tell him as he looked over every visible part of his partner. Lawson's stomach dropped as he ran his hand along his partner's back and down his hindquarters. If anything happened to Kodo...

Lawson couldn't go there without tears threatening. Kodo had been his faithful companion and partner since Lawson's first day in the unit. He would never forgive himself if he'd allowed Kodo to become mortally wounded. Lawson bit back a curse. Blaming himself wouldn't do any good. He knew that on some level. And yet, guilt was building inside him as quickly as a tsunami gained steam in the ocean. Neither seemed stoppable and if Kodo didn't survive, neither would Lawson.

Considering Eileen couldn't remember the last time she'd genuinely let herself cry, the tears spilling down her cheeks now caught her off guard. She'd been emotional and devastated at Kevin's funeral but her eyes had remained dry. It was as though she'd been dehydrated and had no water in her left to use no matter how much she begged for the sweet release of tears.

Not crying had nothing to do with her emotions. She'd been wiped out from Kevin's death, from the loss of the life that never really got off the ground. She'd been gutted at the thought of her son never knowing his father or growing up without someone to go outside and throw a ball with. She'd been crushed that her son would never truly know his father. She'd rubbed her belly and, for better or worse, had decided she would have to be the one to learn to play catch. She would buy a baseball glove and stand out in the front yard if need be. She would sit in the stands and watch all of little Kevin's games, cheering him on.

"Emergency services," the operator began. "Do you need fire, deputy, or ambulance?"

"Deputy," she said. "There's been a bomb on my property. A canine officer is down." Hearing those words out loud nearly cracked her heart in two.

"Okay, ma'am," the operator continued. "Stay on the line while I get help to you. Okay?"

Eileen rattled off her home address and then reiterated the events. She mentioned Lawson Quinn this time, telling the dispatcher that he worked for Austin PD as a canine handler.

"Help is on the way, ma'am," the dispatcher promised. "Is there anyone else at your home?"

Eileen glanced around and saw her neighbors coming out. The look of shock on Millie's face was another gut punch. Eileen exited the Jeep and waved her neighbor back inside. Millie caught on before she turned around and headed back into her home. Cary stood on his porch with a look of shock on his face. If his children caught wind of this, they might use it against him to force a move claiming his neighborhood wasn't safe any longer.

The neighbors, no doubt, had heard the bomb detonate.

Who in the world wanted her dead? Or was someone trying to scare her? Because it was working. Had the perp who'd broken into her home set the bomb? How was that supposed to look like an accident? It also dawned on her the perp had either gotten what he needed or decided to erase her as a potential witness. Either way, it was clear the person wanted her dead.

The thought of little Kevin becoming an orphan before he could sit up on his own slammed into her. The air thinned and she could barely breathe. Who did she have? There was no family to speak of on her side that would be willing or capable of raising her son. Kevin's family would take the baby, but then what? Give her son the same childhood Kevin had had? The one he resented? What about his sister?

Eileen had never felt so alone in the world as to when she thought about what would happen to her baby if she was murdered. Heck, all she had to do was get into an accident or develop a sickness. Where would that leave her son?

Forcing those heavy thoughts aside, she climbed out of the Jeep and ran inside the kitchen where she kept a fire extinguisher. As she retrieved it and bolted toward the now-blazing shed, she thought about how frequently she made a trek out here. She kept her lawn mower inside as well as gardening supplies. This wasn't exactly the time of year for it so the person responsible must have figured out some way to get her to go to the shed. Would there be an 'accidental' fire? She would have investigated a noise given everything that has been going on. Had someone been watching? Waiting? Biding their time until the right moment to strike appeared.

After pulling the pin on the fire extinguisher and dousing the blaze, she ran to Lawson and Kodo. He wasn't standing up, so that had her insides twisted in a knot. Kodo was panting.

"What happened? Where is he hurt?" she asked.

Lawson lifted Kodo enough to reveal a small piece of metal in his side in between a pair of his ribs. There was blood. Blood on the metal. Blood on Lawson's hands. Blood on Kodo and the ground. It dripped but didn't gush, and that was the first positive sign so far. Still, Lawson appeared gutted.

"Let's see if we can stem the bleeding," she said, searching around for something to use.

Lawson shrugged out of his t-shirt, balled it up and gently pressed it against the afflicted area. Kodo twisted in pain and snapped at the air. For a split second, Eileen saw the ripped muscles of Lawson's chest before forcing her gaze back to Kodo's injury.

"I know, buddy," Lawson soothed.

"Help is coming," she said, feeling the exact opposite.

Sirens split the air in the distance. It could be an ambulance or law enforcement, either one. She had no idea who would show first and didn't care. Kodo was the priority either way. He had to be okay. Nothing could happen to him. Nothing permanent. She couldn't lose another thing she cared about. Not now. Not when she was starting to pick up the pieces of her life again.

"You're all right." Lawson's calm voice seemed to relax Kodo enough to keep him from trying to wriggle to standing. The bond between those two sent warmth to her heart. She put a hand on his shoulder and could feel his muscles relax a little with her touch.

As emergency vehicles flooded the scene, all she could do was stay beside Lawson and say a silent prayer Kodo would be all right.

CHAPTER FOURTEEN

"Kodo is going to be just fine. His blood loss has been minimal. He's young and otherwise healthy, and I can repair the damage done by the metal piece in no time back at the office." A local vet by the name of Jack Carlson had shown up with emergency personnel and Lawson couldn't be more grateful. He'd stepped aside to allow the vet to do his work and threw on a shirt while he waited.

Eileen had already given her statement to the deputy who'd arrived on the scene. Lawson was about to give his.

"I can transport Kodo in my vehicle, but I should go now," Dr. Carlson stated with a sympathetic look. He seemed to realize the pain of Lawson needing to stick around to give a statement while his partner was being transported. "I'll keep him comfortable. I promise."

"I'll be there as soon as I can, buddy." Lawson scratched Kodo behind the ears before nodding to Dr. Carlson. Watching his partner as he was being taken away was a gut punch. Eileen walked Dr. Carlson and Kodo to his vehicle, looking just as torn up as Lawson.

"My name is Deputy Hunt and I'd like to hear your account of what happened here this morning." The deputy offered a firm handshake as he stepped into Lawson's line of sight. "I know you're in a hurry to join your partner, so I'll make this as quick as possible."

"I appreciate your consideration. I've already identified myself as Officer Lawson Quinn with Austin PD K-9 Unit," Lawson began before recounting the details of arriving this morning to find someone had been inside the home. He reported that a neighbor had observed a vehicle at the residence and told the tenant, Eileen, during a phone call a few hours ago. For now, he only focused on this morning's event and the possible break-in. He walked the deputy through his observations before giving his statement about Kodo's anxiousness and sudden attention toward the bomb.

The best Lawson could figure was the winds had shifted, causing the scent to blow toward them, where Kodo picked it up. Planting a bomb classified as attempted murder. Lawson mentioned their trip to the bar from last night but didn't go into detail about why they'd gone. He let the officer assume they'd stopped in for a drink.

"Can you classify your relationship to the tenet?" Deputy Hunt asked.

"We're friends," Lawson supplied, forcing a casual tone he didn't feel. Thankfully, the deputy didn't seem to catch on.

"How do you two know each other?" the deputy continued.

"Through friends," he answered. "I knew her husband when he was alive."

The deputy's eyebrow arched.

"We were co-workers, and I promised to look out for his wife. The three of us had been friends first," was the only explanation Lawson intended to give. "What else can I tell you about what happened here?"

The deputy nodded, seeming to realize it was time to move on.

"Anything else you remember," he said. "You know the drill."

"If you have any follow-up questions, feel free to reach out directly to either one of us," Lawson said, offering his personal cell phone number to the deputy, who added it to the report.

"Thank you for your time, sir," the deputy said after finishing up his notes.

"Same to you, Deputy," Lawson stated. Eileen stood at the spot where she'd said goodbye to Kodo. He couldn't imagine the shock she must be in right now.

The deputy finished up his visual inspection of the property before placing crime scene tape around the shed. Lawson had somewhere else to be and he needed to get there as soon as possible. He'd missed an appointment with Jacob. His fellow officer's recent behavior had Lawson feeling uncomfortable. Those pesky hairs on the back of his neck pricked again when he thought about Jacob's hesitation to respond to the earlier text.

Conclusion? Jacob knew something that he wasn't coming clean about. Did Lawson suspect Jacob was a dirty cop? No. He'd always seemed like a standup officer. His reputation was solid at the department. Speculation on officers who were suspect had a way of getting around. Then again, how certain could he be about anything if Kevin was involved in illegal activity and Lawson didn't know it? His confidence flew out the window but not his determination to get to the bottom of what was going on.

Blood on his arms and some still caked on his hands, he fished his cell phone out to see if Jacob had reached out to see why Lawson was late. A report would be issued to his department about his off-duty involvement in the bombing victim's home. Word would get out that he was spending time with Kevin's widow. How would it look? Did he even care at this point?

The short answer? No. All he could think about was Kodo surviving while he got to the bottom of who was behind the bombing. This had gone from poking around to attempted murder. Capital murder considering there were law enforcement officers involved.

He checked the screen to see if any text messages had come in from Jacob. There were several from Jacob asking if Lawson was still coming. And then one asking if Lawson was all right. The department would most likely be in contact as news rolled in as to where Lawson had been and his involvement with this case. Could he spearhead some of the questions by calling his supervising officer and asking for privacy?

Lawson issued a sharp sigh. Not likely. Asking for privacy might make him look guilty and there were going to be a whole lot of questions coming his way now. In fact, while he was still holding his cell phone, his SO was starting to ping messages. He pinched the bridge of his nose with his free hand to stave off the headache trying to form right between his eyes. The blast had been big enough to cause a ringing noise in his ears that didn't want to go away. He was lucky not to have been hit by shrapnel but he would trade places with Kodo in a heartbeat. No question about it.

As a matter of fact, Kodo should be at the vet hospital by now. He would most likely be under anesthesia while being fully examined for more injuries and then stitched up so he'd be good as new. The reassurance his partner would come out on the other side of this ordeal fine had meant the world to Lawson. Healing might take a minute but Kodo would survive. The incident served as a reminder of just how fast someone he loved could be taken, making him also realize how precious time was with the important people in his life.

Shelving the thoughts for now, he walked over to Eileen and then linked their fingers.

"Ready to head downtown?" he asked. It might not be too late to meet Jacob at the coffee shop. Lawson would wait if he had to even though he was itching to get to the vet hospital that was halfway between here and Austin. He'd take the lucky break because they'd been few and far between lately.

"I'm sorry," she immediately said, and he realized she'd been holding back tears.

"None of this is your fault," he reassured, urging her toward the Jeep and away from the scene. She needed time to process what had happened. Getting her away from the shed would give her brain a minute to catch up. She would realize that she wasn't to blame. In fact, she couldn't be more innocent.

"It doesn't feel that way," she said quietly as he deposited her in the passenger seat.

"I know it doesn't," he said, realizing the last thing she needed was someone arguing with her right now. "Just do me a favor and leave the door open for the possibility it will at some point."

After a pause, she gave a small nod. That was all he needed. All she would need too in order to forgive herself.

"Is Jacob still at the coffee shop?" she asked after he reclaimed the driver's seat. He hesitated before closing the door before the realization hit that Kodo wasn't about to jump inside.

Lawson closed the door.

"He sent texts asking where I was and if I was going to show," he said to her as he turned on the ignition and then headed toward the city. The temptation to stop off and check on Kodo was strong, except he'd already kept Jacob waiting too long.

Thinking about what had just happened strengthened his resolve even more. Lawson gripped the steering wheel a little tighter as he navigated out of the neighborhood and onto the highway.

"I can text him back while you drive if you tell me what to say," Eileen offered after a sniffle. She brought her hand up to wipe what had to be rogue tears. Kodo was lucky to have her on his side. Lawson counted himself lucky too. In less than twenty-four hours, his life had flipped upside down and he was a better person for it.

Strangely, he didn't want to go back to the old way of living now. Of course, he needed Kodo by his side.

That was a given. Being with Eileen showed him that he'd been living a half-life. He didn't trust anyone enough to build a real relationship and it needed to change.

"Okay," he said to her. With one hand on the wheel, he fished his cell phone out of his pocket and handed it to her. Their fingers brushed, reminding him of the electrical current that ran between them. "Let him know that I'm on my way. He doesn't want anyone with me, so remember that as you text."

"Will do," was all she said. She seemed to have a new resolve too. Was it possible they were on the same page?

Pretending to be Lawson, Eileen sent a text stating he was on his way. She stared at the screen, waiting for a response.

"Nothing," she said after a few beats of silence.

"It took him a minute to respond to me earlier," Lawson stated. "He might get back to me before I park. Either way, I think we should stop off at the coffee shop."

She checked the time. "I didn't realize it was getting so late in the day. He could be on his lunch break."

"Or on a call," Lawson added.

"Right," she said, "I have no idea what shift he works. I'm so disoriented on time that I didn't even realize we haven't eaten since breakfast at your place."

"I have a couple of power bars tucked into a back-pack if you're hungry," he said. "Or, we can stop off. It isn't like we've heard from Jacob, so I have no idea where he is right now."

"Maybe just a pitstop for tacos or any kind of drive-through would be better," she said. "I'm not usually picky, but power bars sound awful."

Lawson chuckled in a rare break from the heaviness of the day. "After the morning we've had, we can do better."

It seemed like forever ago that her biggest problem was whether or not her husband had been having an affair. Now, she was trying to figure out if he was a dirty cop even though the reality didn't resonate with her. Then again, neither did Kevin cheating. So much for her intuition.

But then, hadn't she known something was up when he'd rarely touched her a few months after the honeymoon? It wasn't natural for newlyweds to sleep apart so much, hardly have sex. Once she got pregnant, he'd used it as an excuse to stop touching her altogether, saying that he wanted her to get her rest plus their different sleep schedules.

He pulled over at the first drive-through taco stand they came across, and then they sat in the Jeep while they ate. Lawson kept his cell phone on his right thigh the entire time and she realized he was waiting on news about Kodo. The relationship between the two of them demonstrated what it was like to truly trust another being and it warmed her heart. Had she ever really trusted any living being?

A voice in the back of her mind said she'd never allowed anyone to get close enough to her after the way her parents treated her.

"How long did the vet say it would take before someone would reach out to you with an update?" she asked.

"He didn't," Lawson said, and she could tell how much the situation weighed on his thoughts.

"Being around Kodo has taught me so much about what had been missing in my life," she said to Lawson.

"How so?"

"The bond you two have is unbreakable," she said. "There's no question either one of you would take a bullet for the other. I'm guessing half the reason you're so frustrated is that you'd rather be the one under a knife if it had to be one of you."

"You're not wrong," he said quietly, and with a reverence that touched her heart so deeply it took a second to catch her breath.

Eileen trusted one person with her life...Lawson. Could she trust him with her heart? Would it make a difference either way? Their attraction had taken on a life of its own, but that didn't mean it would go any further. Could it turn into something real? Something lasting? A growing part of her hoped so.

CHAPTER FIFTEEN

Lawson parked the Jeep a couple of blocks from the coffee shop where he was supposed to meet Jacob. His friend hadn't responded to the text yet, but the bar wasn't open yet, so this was the only play they had at the moment.

"I'll leave the keys with you just in case," he said to Eileen. She leaned over the seat and gave him a sweet kiss.

"Be careful," she said in the kind of warm, soft voice that could melt a glacier during a freeze.

"Same to you," he said. This time, he leaned across the seat and pressed a kiss to her lips. Being with Eileen seemed like the most natural thing, and he was tired of fighting against what they both seemed to want more than air in their lungs.

Looking into her eyes and seeing the concern there, added, "He'll be all right. The confirmation will come through any minute."

"Mind if I get the number to the vet hospital?" she

asked. “I might as well do something productive while I’m sitting here.”

He gave over the information, and she entered it into her cell phone.

“I’ll be right back,” he promised.

She nodded, and it looked like emotion welled inside her. It was almost as though the thought of losing him too would bring her to her knees. There was an inherent risk in Lawson’s job. He couldn’t deny the fact. Being good at his job minimized the dangers. Following protocol reduced it further. Even so, there was no getting it down to zero. Walking outside the door, getting in a car and driving on the highway could result in death.

Four steps away from the door, a text came that Jacob was inside, waiting. *Good.*

The coffee shop was an Austin original. There were walls of windows, wood beams, and more plants than could be found at a nature preserve. The place was small and bustling as he slipped inside and scanned the tables.

Jacob sat toward the front in the corner. Lawson wouldn’t have recognized his friend if he hadn’t leaned back a few moments after Lawson stepped inside. Time to see about getting some answers.

Joining his friend at the small table for two in the corner, Lawson extended a hand. He wanted to measure Jacob’s stress levels based on how moist his palm was. On a scale of one to ten, Jacob was a six.

“Good to see you again,” Lawson started, trying to ease some of the tension between them.

"You too, man," Jacob said as he quickly surveyed the room. "She comes in here before work sometimes."

"Who?" Lawson asked. This conversation seemed off to a running start.

"Liz Fox," Jacob whispered, studying the table like it was a final exam.

"Is that why you decided on this place to meet?" Lawson wondered how long Jacob had been watching key people at the bar. Was he involved?

"Partly," he said then looked Lawson square in the eyes. "Before we go any further with this, I need to know your involvement with Eileen."

"Friends," Lawson said a little more defensively than he'd hoped.

"That all?" Jacob asked, studying Lawson.

"Any reason it's your business?" Lawson fired back.

"It is if my life depends on it...yes."

Fair point.

"Eileen uncovered information about Kevin that seems to be putting her and their newborn in danger," Lawson said, coming clean was the best way to win Jacob's trust. Instinct honed by years of experience had Lawson believing Jacob was innocent. He did, however, know something he was hesitant to share.

"You and Kevin were best friends," Jacob continued.

"At one time," Lawson said. "Yes."

"Mind if I ask what happened?" Jacob asked.

"He got married." It was the absolute truth, so Lawson could say it with one hundred percent conviction. "I'm not involved in anything illegal, and neither is Eileen. She is a single parent who showed up at my door, afraid.

I'll help her in any way I can, in part to honor a promise that I made to Kevin before he died." Lawson saw the tension lines scoring Jacob's forehead ease. "From what we've been able to gather so far, Liz Fox was having an affair with Kevin, and she was possibly blackmailing him into criminal activity that is now coming back on Eileen."

Jacob leaned toward Lawson.

"All right then," he said. "I'd been keeping an eye on the situation with Kevin before he was killed. He was starting to show up at the bar a little too often for someone newly married, which caught my attention in the first place. I confronted him about it once during a shift and he got defensive. Said his marriage might have been a mistake and that he was trying to figure everything out. Said he needed to think, so he came to the bar."

"Did he mention anything about a certain waitress?" Lawson asked.

Jacob shook his head. He pulled out his cell phone, though, and showed a picture of someone with bleached blonde hair and ocean blue eyes.

"I take it that's Liz Fox," Lawson said.

"You've seen her before?" Jacob asked.

"Eileen was approached at the bar last night by a female with ocean blue eyes," he said. "It's not a huge leap to make here."

Jacob nodded.

"Did you ask him straight out if he was having an affair?" Lawson asked.

"Kevin denied it," Jacob said. "He blew up at me, though, and that's when I knew he was guilty."

"Innocent people don't lose their cool in those situations, do they?" The question was rhetorical. They both knew the answer.

Jacob shook his head anyway.

"Did you keep watching him after the blow out?" Lawson asked.

"I had to be more discreet about it, but yes," Jacob said. "The bar has a bad rep. The lead bartender is part owner in the place. His name is Richie Zane. Richie has ties to a biker gang affiliated with trafficking and weapons. There's a meet-up at the bar every few months but I haven't been able to get enough intel to start an official investigation. You know how strapped resources are at the department. Forget about the feds."

Lawson nodded.

"Do you have evidence against Kevin?" Lawson asked. He needed to know the answer even though he didn't want more bad news.

"Nothing other than an affair," Jacob stated. "Which is immoral but not illegal."

"Frequenting a place like the bar doesn't put Kevin's overall behavior in a good light," Lawson said. "I have his laptop, which Eileen gave freely to me. There might be hidden evidence in there."

"I can see about opening an official investigation but cells like these tend to disappear for a while once the heat is on," Jacob pointed out. It was true. They had a network that allowed them to move from place to place when an area got too hot.

"Here's the rub," Lawson began. "I'm avoiding doing anything that could put Eileen's income and benefits in jeopardy. If Kevin was working the wrong side of the law, she could lose everything. It's not like she's living in the lap of luxury, Jacob. I've seen her place. It's a small home in Bixby. She works at a plant nursery and has a four-month-old depending on her."

"I get it," Jacob said. "It's the same reason I convinced myself to look the other way when I should have dug my heels in and investigated while Kevin was still alive."

"If he was dirty, life gets very complicated for his widow," Lawson stated. "She is aware and wants to move forward now that someone has tried to run her off the road. Plus, a bomb detonated at her home a little while ago. It's the reason I'm late. But she doesn't want to tarnish her husband's reputation if he didn't do anything."

Jacob muttered a few choice words.

"You know what happens when baseless accusations like this start being flung around," Lawson pointed out. It wasn't hard these days to ruin a reputation and bring shame on a family before there was evidence to support a claim.

"I've been holding off because I wanted to gather enough evidence to take the whole operation down, not just cut off a leg so I can watch it grow back," Jacob said on a sharp sigh. "But it's been slow moving without Kevin around."

"Did he ever ask you to back off or stay away from the establishment?" Lawson asked.

"No, he didn't."

Those words offered Lawson the first small sign of hope.

A blonde-haired woman in her early thirties strutted right past Eileen as she sat inside the Jeep. The woman caught Eileen's attention in part because she kept looking around as though she feared someone might be following her.

The blonde's gait seemed familiar. There was something else too.

Eileen wouldn't figure out what it was if she sat there. She exited the passenger side as the miniskirt- and combat boot-wearing blonde strode past. The noise made the woman jump. She glanced over, and then her face dropped.

"Excuse me," Eileen said, realizing she'd just found Ocean Eyes. "Liz?"

The woman grabbed onto her shirt as though it was a coat and she was bracing against the cold. Head down, she quickened her pace.

"Ma'am," Eileen said, jogging up beside her. "Please, stop."

The plea went nowhere. The woman kept walking.

"I have a son," Eileen said, stopping. "A bomb went off at my home today. He's innocent and he could be killed."

The server slowed down, then stopped. She turned around. At this distance, Eileen looked into the purest pair of ocean blue eyes.

"You're Liz Fox, right?" Eileen asked.

"We can't talk here," she said, glancing around. "Not out in the open like this."

"Come sit in my Jeep." Eileen didn't wait for a response. She just turned and walked toward the vehicle, praying Liz would follow.

For a split second, Eileen thought Liz would bolt. She would be taking a huge risk in possibly being seen with Eileen.

She climbed in the back seat, left the door open, and waited.

A few seconds later, Liz followed.

"I can't be late to work, so we have to make this quick," the woman said.

"Liz?" Eileen asked for confirmation.

"Yes," she stated. "Fox isn't my real last name, by the way, it's just what I go by on my ID."

Eileen probably didn't want to know exactly what that meant. She had no intention of asking. "Thank you for following me. I know the risk you're taking."

"They were supposed to leave you alone," Liz said, shaking her head. She made a tsk noise as she twisted her fingers together in a braid. "And your little boy. None of this was supposed to reach him."

"I made a mistake," Eileen admitted, sitting almost thigh-to-thigh with her dead husband's mistress. Liz's blue eyes might be beautiful but there was so much loneliness there it was difficult to get past. Up close, she looked older than she probably was. Stress had a way of aging a person. "I called a number."

"Is that what got Richie riled up?" Liz asked.

"It's when things started down a scary path," Eileen explained. "Was my husband...*Kevin*...involved in illegal activity with this Richie person?"

"He thought about it, but, no, not to my knowledge was he involved with the operation," Liz said honestly.

"Are you sure?" Eileen asked. Knowing Kevin had

kept something sacred meant a lot to her. She took it to mean that he cared about his legacy.

"They were hitting him pretty hard," Liz explained. She shot a look of apology before saying, "Richie had caught the two of us in the bathroom." She stopped and cleared her throat. Eileen didn't have to guess what the two of them had been doing in there. Hearing about her husband being with another woman from his mistress was the hardest thing she'd ever done.

"What does that mean?"

"Blackmail," Liz stated plainly. "They knew he was a cop and encouraged me to seduce him once they figured out how much he could benefit them." Another look of apology came. It was almost as though Liz realized for the first time there was a real woman back there somewhere in Kevin's life. "He was cute, and I owed a whole lot of money to Richie when he bailed me out of a bad relationship with..."

Eileen sat there, hands fisted, wishing she could scream.

"Anyway, you don't care about those details," Liz stated before continuing. "Richie thought Kevin was cooperating, so he brought him into the circle a little bit. Kevin kept hemming and hawing about not being able to do something Richie requested. I think it was supposed to show his loyalty. Anyway, Richie got it in his head that Kevin was gathering evidence against every last one of us, but I knew he was trying to keep my name out of it."

"Kevin was trying to protect you from authorities?" Eileen asked, wondering why he hadn't been so concerned about the welfare of his wife and child.

"We got pretty close once Richie forced me to blackmail Kevin, so I told him about the abuse I took in my previous relationship." She shrugged. "I guess he took pity on me and tried to find a way to keep my name out of it."

"What about the note you gave me last night?" Eileen asked.

"That was me trying to protect you and tell you who I was so you would believe me," Liz said. "I didn't want you coming back in the bar. Ever. In fact, I'd hoped you would take the hint and move out of Texas. It's not too late."

Was Kevin's mistress watching out for Eileen? As much as she wanted to hate the woman, it was impossible to when Eileen saw how broken Liz was inside.

"Why go back there?" Eileen asked. "Richie is extorting you too. How long before he does something drastic to make sure you won't be able to testify?"

The questions were valid.

"I have insurance," she said with a satisfied smile. "I recorded everything that has been going on at the bar for the past year and believe me when I say he would go away for life. They aren't the only ones who can blackmail. Anything happens to me, and my landlord has been instructed to come forward with evidence. It's probably the only reason I'm still alive."

"How long before Richie figures it out and goes after your landlord?" Eileen asked.

A visible shiver rocketed through Liz.

"I hope he never does," Liz stated. She checked the smartwatch on her wrist. "But I can't stick around. I'll be late and everyone's nerves are on edge since you showed up at the bar. As it is, I'll have to skip my latte to get to work on time."

"Let me make it up to you," Eileen said. "Or, better yet, let me help you get out of this life. You have the proof we need to bring Richie to justice where he'll be locked behind bars."

"Take him down and his cousin Ronnie is instructed to come after me and you," Liz said.

"I've got news for you," Eileen began, "he already has."

Liz shot a final look of apology before slipping out of the Jeep, and then down the street before she disappeared.

Eileen had felt so close to a breakthrough with Liz, and yet so far. Then, it dawned on her that Liz had most likely been helping Kevin gather evidence against Richie. Eileen had to figure out a way to get Liz to come forward without getting them both killed.

CHAPTER SIXTEEN

"Eileen overheard you arguing with Kevin in her garage. Was it about the affair?" Lawson sized up Jacob and would put his money on his fellow officer being honest about everything he'd seen.

"I almost confronted him about what he was really doing in the bar, to be honest," Jacob said. He was six feet tall, give or take, and had a thick build. He put his elbows on the table and brought his hands up to his face, as though in shame. Or was it regret? Lawson knew all about both.

"But you didn't," Lawson confirmed.

Jacob shook his head.

"I was about to but picked up a bad vibe from him. He'd changed...you know? And I decided that I didn't know him well enough to dig further," he said. "Kevin made BS excuses at first. Claimed there was no way he would cheat on his new wife."

"The affair started digging a hole that he didn't seem able to figure out how to get out of," Lawson recapped.

"Once I realized Kevin was shot because of what he was involved in at the bar, I started treading lightly ever since so I don't end up in a coffin as well," Jacob admitted. "I've got two kids and a wife at home."

"You don't have to figure this out alone any longer," Lawson said. "No one would blame you for walking away altogether if you want to hand over any evidence you've gathered."

"That's the problem, I don't have proof. I have photos of known criminals coming in and out of the back door of the bar, but that's as far as it goes. Other than that, all I have are assumptions and suspicions."

"Fair enough," Lawson said. It seemed they were at a dead end with Jacob. "I might be able to find something on the laptop to help. Kevin had to be keeping the evidence somewhere safe."

"Which leads me to believe it wouldn't be on the laptop," Jacob stated.

"You have a point there," Lawson concluded. Out of the corner of his eye, he saw Military Cut walk through the door. He gave a slight nod toward Jacob, urging him to look over.

Jacob mumbled a curse.

Lawson brought his hand up to finger-comb his hair, using his arm to block as much of his face as possible. Without ordering coffee, Military Cut abruptly turned around and walked out the front door.

"That's not good," Lawson said, all his warning sirens screaming. Both men couldn't get up and out the door fast enough. There were enough people on the street to block their view. Military Cut had slipped into the crowd and was getting away with it.

Lawson had one concern...Eileen.

Activity to the left caught their attention. Eileen was to the right.

"She's in my Jeep, man," was all Lawson said. It was all he had to say.

"I got this guy," Jacob stated, taking off after Military Cut. Lawson bolted right, running so fast and hard that his thighs burned. His lungs clawed for air at this pace, but he didn't care. All he could think about was getting to Eileen and getting her out of danger. The tiny hairs on the back of his neck pricked and his chest squeezed at the thought of anything happening to her. He couldn't lose her, not again.

As he rounded the corner to the parking lot where he'd stashed the Jeep, he saw her in a struggle with a man she'd described as the bartender from last night. Lawson drew his weapon.

"Freeze. Put your hands where I can see them," he demanded.

Richie spun around. Metal glinted against Eileen's neck as she was used as a human shield. A pair of college kids gasped as they turned the corner. They picked up the pace as Lawson instructed them to call 911 and request an officer assist in this location.

"Weapon down," Lawson commanded, thankful Kodo was safe at the vet hospital. He would have charged the perp and could have ended up in far worse condition. Lawson thanked the heavens for small miracles.

"I don't think so," Richie said. The bartender had the kind of body that most would describe as squatty. His arms were like tree trunks despite his otherwise short stature. "Here's what's going to happen. I walk away with this bitch, and you don't follow. Take one step toward us and I slit her throat from ear to ear."

Those words were the equivalent of gut punches.

"Not on my watch," Lawson responded. "As far as I see it, she's all you got keeping you alive right now. You hurt her and you'll die with her."

Without warning, Eileen brought her hand up as fast as an arrow. She connected with Richie's elbow as she spun around. The move caught him off guard and knocked the knife from his grasp. She threw a punch that connected with Richie's jaw. His head snapped back, but he immediately recovered.

"Sonofa—"

Before he could get the word out, he realized that Lawson made a play for the knife. Richie knocked Eileen over with one powerful punch, and then dove for the blade. Richie came up with it a second before Lawson got there.

Both men on the ground, gravel dug into Lawson's shoulder. They fought for his gun after Richie knocked the blade out of reach. Lawson threw a punch that drew blood as it connected with the bridge of Richie's nose. Considering Lawson worked with Kodo now, he was a little rusty at hand-to-hand combat. His partner normally had the perp pinned to the ground or the wall by the time Lawson arrived.

Richie brought his knee up, hitting Lawson's inner thigh. Thankfully, it missed its target, or he would be puking up his insides right now and possibly never having children.

"I know what you did, and I can prove it," Eileen

said, circling them at a safe distance. She'd recovered the knife, but it would be too risky for her to make a move with it and she seemed to realize it.

"Find cover," Lawson managed to bite out. The distraction with Eileen gave Richie a momentary advantage. He threw another punch that felt a lot like slamming Lawson's shoulder into a tree at a hundred miles an hour.

Eileen hesitated as Lawson countered with an elbow to Richie's chin. The bartender's head snapped back. Blood dripped from his nose, but he smiled through the pain. His grip on Lawson's gun hand intensified as the two battled for control.

Rather than risk allowing Richie to take the weapon, Lawson threw another elbow and then chunked the gun. It skidded across the pavement but was safely out of reach.

"Well, isn't that a stroke of luck." A blonde woman took a step forward before bending down and picking up the weapon.

Sirens sounded, but they wouldn't get to the scene in time to stop her from using it.

"Richie, you're a real sonofabitch. You know that?" she said.

"Don't do it, Liz," Eileen warned. "Don't let him drag you to jail too."

Liz seemed unfazed.

"Hands up, jerk," she said to Richie, who was momentarily paralyzed at the realization she would shoot if she got a clear shot. "I said, 'hands up.'"

"You won't shoot me," Richie said, wrestling with Lawson.

The crack of a bullet split the air. Richie tensed as he shouted out in pain. The break allowed Lawson to roll out of the man's grip.

Liz had shot Richie in the ankle. Lawson didn't want to think about how close he'd come to being on the receiving end of a bullet.

"It's time you paid the price for your sins, Richie," Liz said with the kind of anger and grit that had Lawson believing she was about to shoot.

"He's not worth jail time," Lawson said to her. He put his hands out, palms up. "You haven't done anything yet that you can't come back from."

The sirens were practically right on top of them now as Richie grabbed his ankle, curled in a ball.

"You know something," Liz said to Lawson. "You're absolutely right. He's not worth it. But if he makes one move before the cops get here, then I have two witnesses right here that can corroborate the fact I shot in self-defense."

"I'm an off-duty officer, Liz," Lawson continued. "Give me the gun."

Liz looked to Eileen, who nodded.

"Take it before I change my mind," Liz said, meeting Lawson halfway and then handing over the weapon. "I have proof of everything he's done and I'm willing to go to jail too if it means this guy stays off the streets forever."

Lawson retrieved handcuffs from the console of his Jeep, and then placed them on Richie.

"You did the right thing," Eileen said to Liz.

"Yeah? I just wish I'd done it sooner," Liz said to her as the cavalry arrived. "For what it's worth, I'm sorry."

Liz put her hands up as the first officer approached. "I'm ready to come clean."

Jacob came running around the corner.

"I heard there was a gunshot," he said in between gasping for breaths. "It's not you."

"No," Lawson said. "It's not me."

Jacob surprised Lawson with a bear hug.

"We did it," Jacob said. "These jerks are going to jail."

"Yes, they are," Lawson stated as Eileen moved over to them. He glanced at Liz. If she had the proof she said, the courts would use it in exchange for leniency.

"This might sound strange coming from me," Eileen started. "But I hope they go easy on her."

"They will," Lawson reassured. He turned to Jacob. "Can you handle this?"

Jacob nodded.

"I need to check on my partner," Lawson said before linking his fingers with Eileen.

"Go," Jacob said before asking for Lawson's service weapon. Since it had been fired, Lawson had to turn it in. "I'll be sure this is taken care of." Jacob took the gun. "Call in the rest of your statement whenever you're ready."

"Will do." Lawson reached for Eileen's hand. They walked together, fingers linked, to his vehicle. After taking their seats and securing their seatbelts, Lawson asked, "Are you okay?"

"Yes, surprisingly," she admitted as he navigated out of the parking lot and onto the roadway. "After finding out what actually happened with Kevin, I can forgive him and move on. I can't excuse him for having an affair, but I can forgive him. People make mistakes and I want to preserve his memory for little Kevin."

"I think that's a beautiful idea," Lawson said. "And you know what else? You're a beautiful person, inside and out."

"Same with you, Lawson." Those words pierced what was left of his armor. Eileen had made her way into his heart, and he could no longer think about a life without her.

His cell buzzed before he could tell her how he felt.

"Do you mind?" he asked, fishing the phone from his pocket before handing it over to her.

"It's the vet hospital," she said before quickly answering. He shelved the idea of talking to her. Right now, he needed to know Kodo was fine, and she probably needed to hold her son. Besides, it would give him a minute to figure out how to tell her that she'd become the most important person in his life.

Lawson gripped the steering wheel, waiting for word.

"That sounds great," she said, her voice was like sunshine after a monthlong rain. She said a few uh-huhs into the phone before ending the call.

"What did they say?" Lawson asked before she had a chance to return his cell.

"That Kodo is stitched up and doing beautifully," she informed. Those words were a sonnet and her voice was music to his ears. "They want to keep him overnight and said he's medicated so you should take the night off. Local volunteers have lined up to sit with him and make certain he has everything he needs. He'll be ready to come home tomorrow."

Relief was a tsunami, crashing down hard on Lawson. He sniffed back a tear and realized how much tension he'd been holding since his partner had been injured.

"I hope they open early," he said. "Because I plan to be there the second the doors open to take my boy home."

"Good," she said. "Because I plan to be right there beside you when you do."

They both seemed to exhale. For the rest of the ride to Bixby, they talked about little things like the weather. Conversation moved onto how much Eileen couldn't wait to introduce Lawson to her son.

A strange feeling overcame Lawson. One he couldn't readily identify. Was he nervous about meeting a baby?

He chuckled because the answer was yes. And in a few minutes, he would come face to face with the other important male in Eileen's life.

CHAPTER SEVENTEEN

Millie walked over and handed little Kevin to Eileen. She'd greeted them the second they'd pulled up outside. It was dark and she was hungry. But there was something important she needed to take care of.

"Lawson, this is my son," she said. She could feel herself beaming.

"Hey there, little guy," Lawson said. He looked up at Eileen with absolute wonder in his eyes. "He's a tiny thing. And perfect. Can I hold him?"

Eileen fought back the emotions threatening to suck her under at the thought of Lawson holding little Kevin. "Yes. Of course. Here." She leaned toward him as he cradled his arms.

"I've never done this before," he said.

"You look like a natural to me," she reassured. He did. Seeing the two of them together like that gave her chills and made her believe in families again.

Lawson bounced a little as he took a couple of steps

away from the two of them, talking to little Kevin about his father.

"Thank you," Eileen said to Millie, thinking she would never be able to repay her neighbor for her kindness.

"You're the daughter I should have had, Eileen," Millie said, looking her square in the eyes. "You don't have to keep thanking me. Plus, I plan on being in yours and this little guy's lives for as long as I'm alive. So, you can save all the *thank you*s until the end when I can no longer walk, and I need someone to pump me up." Millie smiled despite her eyes welling with tears. "I'm just thankful this whole mess if over and both you and little Kevin are fine." She paused for a second like she was trying to get a handle on her emotions. "I don't know what I would do without you two now that you've wormed your way into my heart."

"You'll never have to find out," Eileen reassured. "I'm afraid you're stuck with both of us for life."

"Is that a promise?" Millie asked with a wink. A stray tear escaped and slid down her timeworn cheek.

"You're the mother I never had, Millie," Eileen said. She was speaking the truth. Her own mother didn't have the time of day for her and didn't seem to notice that she had a grandson. At the end of the day, Eileen couldn't fault her mother. The woman had suffered a horrible tragedy in losing her firstborn. As much as Eileen would like to believe she would have reacted differently, she didn't know for certain. No one did. Only those few people who'd lost a child could relate to each other. One thing was certain, Eileen had been carrying around the burden of her parent's rejection far too long. It was time to let go and step into her future. "And you're the family I'd like to claim."

After all, blood didn't always make a family. Some were chosen by the heart and pasted together with love.

"It would be an honor to be considered your mother," Millie said, more of those tears leaking out of her eyes. "Even more to be called Mimi Millie by your little angel when he gets old enough to speak."

"Mimi Millie?" Eileen said with a warm smile. "Sounds like you've been thinking about this for a little while."

"I have," she said, "and I've been meaning to bring up the subject but didn't want to overstep my bounds. I know you do have a mother."

"Not really," she said. "I'll always love the person who brought me into this world, and I've decided to forgive her whether she deserves it or not. But I'm not sitting around and waiting for her to call any longer. If she wants to be in my life, fine. I'd never refuse her. We all make mistakes and should be given second chances as long as we don't keep hurting the people we are supposed to love. Then, I'll wave from a distance and protect my heart and the hearts of the ones I love." She couldn't help herself but to glance over at Lawson at that moment.

"He's a good one," Millie said.

"You've hardly been around him," Eileen pointed out. "How do you know so quickly?"

"When you get to be my age, you figure folks out after being in the same room with them for a minute," Millie explained. "They open their mouth and I can tell you what's about to come out with a whole lot of folks.

Those people who think they're slick, aren't. It gets real difficult to pull the wool over my eyes when I've seen just about every type of person out there." She flicked her eyes at Lawson. "Some are just made of good and shouldn't be let go."

"That's not exactly up to me," Eileen said to Millie. "But I appreciate the feedback."

"I've seen the way he looks at you," she said, wrinkling her face like she'd just bit into a pickled prune. "I'd be an idiot not to notice the man has it bad for you."

"Doesn't mean he's ready to go the..." She stopped herself. The attraction between her and Lawson was real. It was noticeable to her, so it shouldn't surprise her that others had picked up on it. An attraction could fizzle out. Plus, he hadn't mentioned the two of them being anything other than friends. Lawson seemed fond of little Kevin but that didn't mean he wanted to be an instant father. And if that wasn't enough, Eileen had her hands full with the nursery and a baby. Little Kevin was barely more than four months old. "Besides, I have little Kevin and no time to work dating into my life right now."

"Who said anything about dating?" Millie quipped. Then, she slowed her smile. "You know, I lost a husband too. We had a beautiful life but there were times when it was overwhelming that we couldn't have children. Both of us had a picture in our head of little ones running around." She smiled warmly at the memory. "Big holiday parties and years of diapers. Between my uterine fibroids and his low sperm count, we didn't have much of a chance even though that didn't stop us from trying. For years after we found out that our chances of having kids were next to nil, we would get melancholy every time we heard a little one cry while out to dinner or at the grocery."

"Your heart is so big. Did the two of you ever consider adopting or infertility treatments?" Eileen asked, hoping she wasn't overstepping any bounds. Then again, they'd taken their relationship from friendship to family, so she figured she was okay.

"Of course," Millie responded. "We thought about every option available and decided children weren't in the cards for us. Once we got over the hump and reimagined our life, we were fine. There's more than one path in life. Once we realized the two of us were family enough for each other, we moved on. Nathan is the one who noticed that I could grow pretty much anything I wanted without trying. We decided I was meant to nurture a different kind of living being. So, we started the business and never looked back."

The smile on her face every time she talked about Nathan caused Eileen's heart to squeeze. She hoped to find a love like theirs someday.

"Someone is trying to get your attention," Millie said with a mischievous smile.

Eileen's heart squeezed a second time when she turned and locked eyes with Lawson.

The minute Lawson's gaze connected with Eileen's, it was like time warped. They were suddenly back in the honky tonk bar seeing each other for the first time. A stray lightning bolt hit him square in the chest as she walked toward him. Millie came over and took the baby from his arms.

"What happens next with Kodo?" she asked with so much compassion his heart took another severe hit. They were racking up.

"He'll be transported home tomorrow where I'll take care of him and see to it that he heals properly," he stated. "It's time for him to retire and there's no way I'm giving him up. I'll do whatever it takes to make sure that I'm the one who gets to adopt him. His service is done. He did good. And now, it's time for him to be spoiled rotten."

"No one deserves it more than Kodo," she seemed to agree. "He's warming up to me."

"Who couldn't love you?" Lawson said before he could reel the words back in. He could feel his cheeks heat to a hundred and ten degrees, so he backtracked. "All I mean to say is that the two of you have forged a bond. He's not like that with most people."

"Then he has good taste," she said with a smile that lit half a dozen campfires inside him. It also made him want to reach out to her and claim those pink lips of hers, mark her as his while she did the same. He wanted to be hers.

There was no denying an attraction between the two of them. Could it go somewhere real? Because he had no interest in doing a casual fling with Eileen. Plus, he highly doubted she would want that anyway.

"Yes, he does," he finally said. "And I'd like to think the same for me."

"Does that mean you like me?" she said with a spark in her eyes that bordered on need.

"I'm afraid that I'm a lot worse off than that," he finally admitted. "I'm in love with you, Eileen. I knew the minute I saw you two years ago that you were special, and it scared the daylights out of me. I'm not proud of stepping aside like I did, but I didn't know if I could love you in the way you deserved. At least Kevin wanted to try. I can't fault for him that. Couldn't then, either. Even though, every single time I saw you, all I could think was that should be me standing next to you, kissing you, loving you."

She blinked up at him but compressed her lips like she was holding back what she really wanted to say, which made him nervous as all get-out. It didn't matter, though. This time, he wasn't letting her walk away without knowing her options and just how much he'd fallen in love with her.

"Did you say *love*?" she asked, not bothering to cover the shock in her voice.

Lawson took in a breath. Here he was, about to throw himself out into the deep end. No regrets this time. No looking back.

"If all you want is friendship from me, you have it," he finally said. "But I have a whole lot more to give. I'm in love with you and I'd like to be a family." He took a knee before taking hold of her hand. He studied the delicate skin of her wrist before braiding their fingers together. He feathered a kiss on each of her knuckles. "You should know that I'm hoping for a whole lot more."

"How much more?" she asked with a smile as bright as the stars and wide as the sun.

"All of you," he said without hesitation. "And I'd like to give all of me in return. I want to spend my life waking up next to you however long we get. I'm banking on a lifetime, but we can take this road one day at a time. And if you'd do me the incredible honor of marrying me, I would like to be little Kevin's father. Not just in name and not to replace the memory of Kevin. I'd like to step in for the assist and teach this kid what a great person his father truly could be."

Eileen was already nodding before he finished his sentence. Tears streamed down her beautiful cheeks. "I can't wait to marry you, Lawson."

He stood up and pulled her into an embrace.

"I want to spend the rest of my life loving you," she continued. "Little Kevin couldn't ask for a better person to step in and raise him. And a small part of me thinks Kevin might be smiling down on this moment from wherever he is."

"He can rest now," Lawson said. "I'll take it from here and make him proud."

"I love you, Lawson," she said.

He pressed a kiss to her lips as he realized he'd found the only home he ever needed. With little Kevin and Kodo, their family was complete. And if she was game, he wouldn't mind trying for a girl.

CHAPTER EIGHTEEN

Epilogue

A ghost sat in the bed at Uncle T.J.'s ranch, not Archer Quinn. Lawson took a step inside the bedroom door and then tightened his grip on Eileen's hand. Millie was in the sitting room with little Kevin and Kodo was protecting them both.

"Dad," Lawson began as his father opened his eyes. "This has been a long time coming and I know you asked for everyone to be in the room before you spoke, but I'd like to say a few words before everyone gets here, if that's all right with you."

Archer swallowed hard and then gave a small nod. He looked like he tensed up to take a punch or a bullet, which hit Lawson square in the chest. He wasn't here to shame his father or make him feel awful for past mistakes. Life was too short to worry about past wrongs. Today, the future, that's where Lawson wanted to put his energy.

"This beautiful woman beside me has agreed to do me the great honor of becoming my wife," he said before planting a kiss on the back of Eileen's hand. "I wanted the two of you to meet and to tell you that I fully expect you to be sitting in the front row as the father of the groom.

His father didn't immediately speak. Instead, tears welled in his eyes. The infection delivered a blow, but the doctor had said Archer Quinn was a fighter.

"I'm Eileen. It's a pleasure to meet you, sir." She stepped forward to offer a hand as Archer shook his head.

"Not sir," he said. It seemed to take a lot of energy to speak. "Dad."

Well, now Lawson's eyes were watering up.

"Dad, it is," Eileen said as she leaned in for a light hug. "I hear you're getting stronger every day."

Dad smiled.

"You should have seen me last week. I was a sight," he said and then coughed.

Being back on the ranch caused so many memories to flood Lawson. He'd shoved out the good. Why was it so easy to remember the bad?

"We have a son," he continued. "His name is Kevin. I plan to adopt him, and his name will be Kevin Houston-Quinn to honor his father, who passed away."

Dad's smile grew as he nodded again.

They agreed to keep Houston in the baby's last name in honor of his father. Kevin made his mistakes, but everyone had good and bad in them. No one was perfect or immune to messing up. So, Eileen and Lawson planned to bring little Kevin up knowing who his father was—the good sides of Kevin—and part of Kevin's family in Louisiana. Turned out after they dug into his e-mail that Kevin was not just hiding an affair, but his younger sister had gotten involved in something shady and he was trying to help her out of it. He was juggling the past and his future, and it all came crashing down around him. The stress got to him, and he screwed up royally. In the end, though, he was trying to figure out how to make it right. How to make his mistakes go away and how to figure out a way to deserve the woman he'd married and the child on the way.

"I'm proud of you, son," his father managed to say.

"You have no idea what it means to hear you say those words, Dad."

A knock at the door was followed by Griff and his bride Laurel entering with a cooler full of cold beers. Harding and Naomi entered next, helping themselves to a cold one. Barrett and Connie walked in with huge smiles on their faces, followed by Crawford and Virginia. Everyone took either a beer or a sparkling water.

Griff brought one of the latter to their father.

Normally, Griff was the one who made the big speeches and grand gestures, but this time Lawson took the floor.

"I think that I speak for everyone here when I say that we can't wait to go fishing together once you lick this infection and heal all the way from the cancer," he said. His brothers and sisters-in-law raised their drinks high in the air. "The doctor reassured everyone that your prognosis is good, and you should live a very long time once you get past this health blip." Lawson paused. "Which is a very good thing because we all have plans, some of us have families or are ready to start them, and we all agree that we want you to be part of our lives."

"It would be an honor," Dad said, raising his sparkling water.

"We've all had some kind of recent reminder that life can turn on a dime. There are no guarantees and instead of looking at that as a bad thing, we've decided to choose to see it as a reminder to live every day like it's the last."

"Here. Here," Griff stated.

"All is certain is that everyone in this room would like it very much if we all went back to being a close-knit family again," Lawson stated. They needed to take care of each other and really be there for each other.

"I'm already imagining big holidays with more food than anyone could possibly eat in one sitting," Dad said.

"And Sunday suppers. We should bring those back," Barrett added as heads nodded and 'whoops' could be heard.

"Then, it's settled," Lawson agreed.

Isaac and Noah popped their heads inside. "We heard a party going on in here. Mind if we join you?"

"Family is always welcome here," Dad said.

"Good thing because there's a whole bunch of us and we can't wait to be a true family again," Isaac said.

"To family," Griff stated, handing out more drinks as the rest of their cousins filed in the room. When everyone had something in hand, Griff said, "I can't think of better people to spend the rest of my life around."

"Cheers," came in unison.

Conversation lasted until Archer's eyelids got too

heavy to stay open. It was the happiest Lawson had seen his father in longer than he could remember.

When his little family walked outside into the sun, he told her all about his plans for big Christmases and family dinners. Eileen's eyes lit up and she said that had a few plans of her own. They involve giving little Kevin a baby brother or sister. Then, she stopped long enough to ask him about Millie. They'd become close and she didn't want to leave her in a lurch. Lawson reassured her that Millie would never be left behind. She was family too. And he wanted her to meet his father.

Millie had told Eileen that at her age, she didn't need romance but that she wouldn't turn down a best friend. They both seem to have the same idea to introduce her to Archer, so they smiled.

"You can keep working at the nursery or doing whatever you want," Lawson said. "I would never get in the way of what makes you happy. I want you to know that."

"There is a little project that I'd like to start working on right now." She looked into his eyes and then kissed him as she wrapped her arms around his neck. "I'll be busy with little Kevin, my job, and planning our wedding."

"Really?" he asked. "Because I'd like to skip right to the honeymoon."

Lawson looked at Eileen, really looked at her. He was the luckiest man alive.

CHAPTER NINETEEN

BONUS - Excerpt from COWBOY RECKONING

The sun was descending on what had been a scorching hot late summer day in Cattle Cove, Texas. Ensley Cartier had parked her car on the side of the road. She walked through the woods and entered the meadow; the beautiful oak trees a stark contrast to the memory of what had happened here.

This place. This beautiful and destructive place had taken so much from her. An icy chill ran down her spine at the memory of her younger brother walking into these woods years ago and never walking out.

Coming back to her old hometown, she'd felt compelled to stop here first. What had happened here was the reason she'd come back to town anyway.

The trail that had led to the meadow was overgrown. The same path had been well-worn years ago. A lot had changed since those innocent days in high school when her future had been bright, and she didn't have to leave the light on to sleep at night.

It was getting late and she shouldn't be out here

alone. That creepy feeling she'd heard referred to as a cat walking over a grave caused her skin to goosebump.

Ensley turned tail and picked up her pace. Her hiking boot got caught on scrub brush and she nearly face-planted. She corrected her balance, grabbing hold of a tree trunk as her phone went flying and the sharp bark jabbed into her palms. She mumbled a curse.

Thankfully, her flashlight was still on and she could plainly see her phone. Getting from point A to point B was another story altogether. As she slowly stepped toward the glowing light, a noise stopped her cold.

A twig snapped behind her. Icy chills raced up her spine as she reminded herself this was deer country. Though there were probably other creatures out here that she didn't want to consider.

The hair on her arms pricked as the feeling of being watched settled over her.

Heart thundering in her chest, Ensley made a move for her cell phone, snatched it and then ducked behind a tree. She could only pray that whatever was behind her couldn't hear her out-of-control heartbeat against her ribs.

Her cell picked that moment to buzz, indicating an e-mail came through. She squeezed her hand around the speaker a few seconds too late. If there was a person behind her, there was no way he or she wouldn't have heard the noise.

Then again, the woods were alive with sounds from cicadas chirping to crickets to frogs. The wind whistled through the trees. She was grateful for the breeze in what otherwise would've been a stifling hot night.

On all fours, Ensley heard the first low and deep

growl. It was the deep baritone of an animal that was close by and ready to strike. She scrambled to stand, fingers closed around her cell phone. She shone the light in the direction of the growl in time to see an incredible, massive German shepherd.

To keep reading, click here.

ALSO BY BARB HAN

Don't Mess With Texas Cowboys

Texas Cowboy's Protection

Texas Cowboy Justice

Texas Cowboy's Honor

Texas Cowboy Daddy

Texas Cowboy's Baby

Texas Cowboy's Bride

Texas Cowboy's Family

Texas Cowboy Sheriff

Texas Cowboy Marshal

Texas Cowboy Lawman

Texas Cowboy Officer

Texas Cowboy K9 Patrol

Cowboys of Cattle Cove

Cowboy Reckoning

Cowboy Cover-up

Cowboy Retribution

Cowboy Judgment

Cowboy Conspiracy

Cowboy Rescue

Cowboy Target

Crisis: Cattle Barge

Sudden Setup

Endangered Heiress

Texas Grit

Kidnapped at Christmas

Murder and Mistletoe

Bulletproof Christmas

For more of Barb's books, visit www.BarbHan.com.

ABOUT THE AUTHOR

Barb Han is a USA TODAY and Publisher's Weekly Bestselling Author. Reviewers have called her books "heartfelt" and "exciting."

Barb lives in Texas--her true north--with her adventurous family, a poodle mix and a spunky rescue who is often referred to as a hot mess. She is the proud owner of too many books (if there is such a thing). When not writing, she can be found exploring Manhattan, on a mountain either hiking or skiing depending on the season, or swimming in her own backyard.

Made in United States
North Haven, CT
15 August 2022

22740381R00108